Packing Smack, Talking Wombats

Steve Tolbert's other young adult books are

Channeary
Settling South
Stepping Back
Eyeing Everest
Escape to Kalimantan
Tracking the Dalai Lama
Dreaming Australia
Surfing for Wayan
O'Leary, JI Terrorist Hunter

For further information go to www.southcom.com.au/~stolbert

Steve Tolbert

Packing Smack, Talking Wombats

Acknowledgements

Lyrics from 'I'm Waitin' For The Man' and 'Heroin' are from *The Best Of The Velvet Underground: Words and Music of Lou Reed* – Polygram Records, distributed in Australia by Verve.

Lyrics from 'Songbird' are from Eva Cassidy's *Songbird*, distributed in Australia by Didgeridoo Records.

The quote from Shakespeare's *As You Like It* is taken from *The Dictionary of Quotations & Proverbs, The Everyman Edition*, p. 216, Octopus Books, London.

Pacvking Smack, Talking Wombats
ISBN 978 1 74027 407 4
Copyright © text Steve Tolbert 2007
Cover image: Jennifer Arthur

First published 2007
Reprinted 2016

GINNINDERRA PRESS
PO Box 3461 Port Adelaide 5015
www.ginninderrapress.com.au

PROLOGUE

Patriarch Inlet, remote east coast of Flinders Island

Two plain-clothes officers sat on the lounge suite in front of him with glum, sympathetic looks on their faces.

'Mr Cassidy,' the one on the left said, 'the reason we're here is because something tragic has happened.' His eyes turned bloodshot and swelled. Red tears seeped down his cheeks.

What the officer said next sent him screaming and he woke breathless, his heart pounding. No one around: nothing but the empty shack, the grey dawn and a seagull squawking and walking on the roof.

'Dawn's the best part of the day, don't you reckon?' Santi asked in his mind, after he settled.

Her blend of Indonesian accent and Aussie idiom made him smile. 'Uh huh.'

She burrowed closer, pressing herself against him. 'Care to start the morning off with a bang, Pete?'

'I could be coaxed.'

'Good.' She ran a hand down his stomach, kissing his neck and cheek, before more seagulls landed on the roof, strutting over him emitting low caws and piercing cries.

Memory flight stalled, he got up and went over to the kitchen window and watched the rising sun spread light over the sea and sky. 'Ready to go?' he asked his boys after a while.

Outside he used the loo, then grabbed the fishing gear and rock-hopped down to a granite platform sheltered by great boulders jutting out of the water. He fished there, talking to John and Joshua about the size of the swell and where the rips were working.

After breakfast he filled his daypack with binoculars, water, bread,

Vegemite, a thermos of coffee and a book entitled *Birds of the Furneaux Islands*, then wound his way down to the shoreline.

His daydreams strengthened. While John and Joshua surfed, he and Santi joined the other walkers and joggers moving along the water's edge. 'The beach is a beauty,' she'd say then. And there was the swing of her hair, the shine in her eyes and those small, dark breasts loosely haltered as a concession to Gold Coast beach fashion. Not a bikini ever made that could improve on hers.

A flock of small birds flew over and turned as one towards the sea. They twisted, swept upwards, then returned in a flash to settle on the beach not far away. 'Chit-chit-chit,'they sounded, as they bill-probed the sand for food.

'Red-necked stints, Santi,' he called out.

Moments later came, 'Tee-tee-tee.' These birds stood motionless on toothpick legs.

'Sandpipers.'

'Bibi-bibi-bibi.'

He used his binoculars to spy on the largest of the shore birds moving into a swarming mass of soldier crabs. 'Whimbrels getting their full feed near the waterline."

Past Patriarch Inlet the great numbers of birds thinned, but whorled shells grew plentiful.

'We'll look for two or three of the best ones and take them back with us,' he said to her. The delicate, white-ribbed nautilus shells kept him stooped over the longest. 'Aren't they magnificent? It's like they once housed huge sea snails.' He picked one up and peered into its wide mouth. 'There's a shop in Whitemark that sells these,' he said, wrapping it up in a rag and adding it to the others in his daypack.

He continued past a small headland and another lagoon before veering into the low scrub, where he intruded on a wombat then almost stepped on a small tiger snake slithering out of its circle of sunlight. He backed off and found another clearing out of the wind, where he unpacked and sat down and started eating his lunch. Skinks blended in with the soil here. Insects buzzed him. Honeyeaters and rosellas flitted amongst the melaleuca and banksia trees. Time slowed. And for the first time since leaving the shack, he lost his family. Heart racing, he packed up quickly. To find them again, he had to get back out there on the shoreline and keep walking and talking to them, because all he was made of was memory and all he wanted to remember was their Gold Coast holidays.

Returning to his shack late in the day, he stopped and used his binoculars to search Babel Island propped up on the horizon. Drawing a bead closer in, he saw them skimming the ocean, dipping and darting fast heading towards that island. 'See them out there? Mutton-birds,' he said, pointing. 'They mate for life, you know, and always fly back to the same burrow.'

The tide swept in. Wavelets foamed white around his calves. He watched those birds until they disappeared like all the other seabirds had for the day.

Fatigue hit him hard then. Life in the flesh went bleak again. He left the water and plopped down on the sand. The sea and sky dimmed. The breeze died away. In the silence, everything was reduced to his breathing and pulse, before a cold emptiness swept through him and he started to shiver. He got up and headed back to the shack. Once inside again he lit up the lantern that hung down from a hook in the middle of the roof, then moved to the sink, asking Santi for instructions on making the soup. She answered and stayed close. Moments later the boys ducked in asking when tea would be ready.

The smells of kerosene and food soon filled the shack but, as the long night drew in, his family's voices grew fainter, no matter how much he relived with them what they'd done that day.

After eating and washing dishes and clothes and filling up the water jug again, there was nothing more to do, so he poured himself a mug of tea, lay down on his bed and listened to the lantern hiss and the roof creak as the air outside cooled. He tried to read, but he couldn't get through more than a few lines before his mind wandered. Frustrated, he stared up at the ceiling and slid his gaze along its cracks to the seam where the ceiling met the wall. He fixed his eyes on the dusty spiders' webs and their trapped husks that filled the shadowy gaps there. Thinking about those husks – how long they'd been there and how long he could be under them every – sent his body cold again.

He got up and turned off the lantern. Darkness was coffin-like. He curled up on his bed hoping sleep would follow. It didn't: only his intruding memories did as they travelled restlessly from the Gold Coast to Blackall and back again. He tried to divert them by concentrating on Santi undressing. Slipping out of her panties. Sitting down on the edge of the bed. Smiling over at him. Unclasping her bra. Loosening her hair and letting it flow down her narrow back. Donning her silk nightgown, sliding in next to him and moving those long-fingered hands over him. Here, in the middle of nowhere in the middle of the night, he ached to really feel her touching him, her skin warm against his. He grew desperate trying to find her. He wanted to tell her about plans he had for walking up to Northeast River. About how they could do up the shack. About how they could sell nautilus shells to the shop in town. And what about this idea: go into Whitemark and buy a cray ring and spend more time on the rocks in the morning catching crays before heading off along the beach?

Santi drifted in, drifted out, but never stayed long enough to carry his mind away from the room pressing in on him. His memories betrayed him. They refused to offer her up close, uninterrupted – her arms around him, her legs moving over his, her voice soft, her breathing building.

Locked up in his solitude, he felt lonelier than he ever thought possible. A wave of panic hit him. Jumping out of bed, he groped for his torch and burst out the back door. There were diversions out there: the moon, wavelets lapping, stars falling across the sky. And gradually, they settled him down. An hour later, he returned to the shack with the sea in his ears and flopped down on the bed and slipped into dream-filled sleep.

He screamed and woke again to a squawking seagull over him. Minutes later, dawn light made the place big again; big enough for his daydreams that loomed up clear and strong for another day.

'Dawn's the best part of the day, don't you reckon, Pete?'

He still did, yes. But the nights and that officer with the bleeding eyes were making him pay for each one of them.

1

'I can't, Mum. I'm meeting Ben at Zep's Café in half an hour. I'll be late.'

Jackson's mother gave her a scorching look. 'Mild crayfish curry. It's David's favourite. You know that. What am I supposed to do, use soy milk and shrivelled-up lettuce leaves instead?'

'You could feed him maggot soup for all he cares!'

Even the goldfish was in on it now, ogling them through its bowl on the sink, its blood pressure surely soaring as well.

Jackson took a deep, calming breath. 'Mum, David comes here for you, not for your five-star wines and silver-service meals.'

Her mother barely listened. 'Please, dear,' she beseeched her. 'Listen, Chung's is just around the corner from Zep's.' She grabbed her handbag, took out a fifty-dollar note and stuffed it in Jackson's jeans pocket, her desperation taking no account of budgetary restraint. 'Buy the coconut milk and coriander for me, then put it in a taxi and send it home. Easy. You get to Zep's on time and I've got what I need here. Please.' She waited, the success of her night hanging on her daughter's decision – well, in her mind, anyway.

On countdown to Ben-time, only twenty-six minutes remained. Her mother's eyes, and the stupid goldfish's, stayed fastened on her. To 'just around the corner' her mother should have added 'and a couple of hundred metres further on'. Also, empty, extremely short-haul taxis weren't easy to come by in St Kilda this time of night. But the thing was, she couldn't remember the last time she'd said 'no' to her mother, especially when David was involved.

'Ooooh, all right!' she cried out, grabbing her jumper and sprinting for the door.

She got to Fitzroy Road in record time – nine minutes. Panting like some dying beast from the effort, Jackson paused to let her lungs recover. As Zep's was close, she decided to see if Ben was there early. She hadn't walked far before she spotted him – daypack in hand – crossing the road and entering the alleyway next to the Criterion Hotel. She checked her watch: still fourteen minutes to go; not that Ben was a stickler for meeting her on time. She relaxed, turned and headed for Chung's.

Mother catered for, Jackson arrived at Zep's two minutes late. She took a seat at an outside table and waited for Ben.

Time passed. Tables filled. She told the waitress twice that she was waiting for someone.

Finally she got up and crossed the road. The alley was blacked out beyond the red-neon-lit entryway.

'Ben,' she called, barely raising her voice. With all the traffic roaring by he'd have to be close to hear her, but if she called any louder she'd attract attention.

She stepped nervously into the darkness, running her hand along the building like a blind woman. The stench of urine and decaying rubbish struck her first, and she soon sensed it seeping into her hair, skin and clothes. She stopped and looked back at the glaze of headlights. A tram rumbled past. Moments later a cat yowled just metres away.

She squatted down and whispered, 'Puss, puss.' If she could draw it closer, she might be able to stroke it and divert her mind from her fear. 'Puss, puss.'

But the cat stayed hidden away until it yowled again, coming into view at the entryway. There it sat, as if it owned the place, and watched the traffic flash past.

Watching the cat settled her. She gazed into the blackness and worked her way back six months to the day she and Ben first met on the bike track.

Having survived her last blade ride before mid-year exams started, she was hot and thirsty and her ankles ached, so she flopped down on a bench taking little notice of the boy already sitting there.

'Straight swap,' he said loudly, after she was in her bare feet and had drained her water bottle. Sitting with his arm dangling over the back of the bench, a walkabout headset plugged into his ear, words spilled out. 'Your roller blades for this top-of-the-range, twenty-seven-speed, alloy-wheeled mountain bike that's the exact replica of the one Sean Healy rode to win this year's Thredbo Mountain Bike Classic.' He nodded once to indicate the bike next to him. 'But you've only got five seconds to decide.' He started to count.

She eyed him quizzically, seeing herself reflected in his wraparound mirror sunnies. 'Done.' Grinning, she tossed over her worthless blades and waited for him to get serious.

He didn't, but just detached his headset and kept on talking. 'Great. I'm Ben. Twenty, still wrinkle free, owner of a partially restored FJ Holden ute, the latest in digital camera–mobile phone technology, and with a big interest in just about everything else quality-made in life.' Dimples punctured his cheeks. His smile was a Colgate ad. 'So besides being a proud new owner of a five-star bike, who are you?'

A tiny laugh, like a hinge creaking, escaped her lips. 'Jackson.' Her eyes dropped to her feet. 'Eighteen and foot-wrinkled like an old turtle.'

She stopped, not prepared to go any further, for the moment anyway.

'Jackson. Like in Michael?'

'No. First name. Like in Pollock. My mother is, or was, an artist.'

His eyes dulled. Artists – quality-made or not – had obviously missed his big interest list.

He stood up, wheeled the bike over and pressed his smile button again. 'Regarding the wheels, just one proviso.'

'What's that?'

'There's a twenty-four-hour trial period for sampling the merchandise,' he said, glancing down at his joggers.

They were obviously thinking the same thing: excluding a partial amputation, how was he ever going to get his feet into her blades?

'We meet here tomorrow, same time, to either finalise, change or otherwise cancel the arrangement.'

This intrigue, from out of nowhere, and so timely. Her worries about mid-

year exams eased back a notch. But unlike those exams, Jackson doubted 'the arrangement' could go on much longer. Gleaming in its newness, the bike appeared to be everything he said it was. A chancy ploy for a second meeting, which was what he had to be up to.

'You trust that I'll be here?'

'I'd like to.'

She got up and gripped the handlebars firmly as a test of transferred ownership, her face close up in his sunnies. The parts of him she could see were impressive. A half head taller than her, tanned, broad-jawed, wavy honey-gold hair dropping over his forehead and ears, one with a small gold ring in it.

'We'll just have to see what tomorrow brings or doesn't bring then, won't we?' she said, her skin starting to warm again.

'We will.'

To her surprise, he turned and walked off with her blades.

Of course she was there to meet him the following day, and for the rest of the week after that. His script and the intrigue stayed the same: the most casual bench-sitting pose in all of St Kilda, dimple perforated smile, sunnies' reflections, more twenty-four-hour trials. She swapped the bike for a gold watch, the watch for a small laptop and the laptop for a new set of awesome, ice-blue N-DORFIN 2 roller blades.

'You can have your old ones back for spares if you like,' he quipped, enjoying himself in uninterrupted dimple time.

'No thanks.' So who was he anyway? Cat burglar? Swap meet specialist? Photographer model? She asked him finally.

'I was wondering the same about you,' he answered, coyly. 'Why don't we go the next step to learn more about each other? Come out with me, Jackson. Back here for sunsets. Then to cafés, clubs, a barbie party or two. Give it a few weeks, then if either of us has any questions, we can ask and fill in what we've missed.'

She'd liked the way he used 'we' then, so his mystique — augmented by his film star looks, his big interest list enthusiasm and love making style — stayed strong for a time. While it did, her girlfriends agreed that St Kilda housed no one else quite like him. And judging by their hungry stares after school each day, when Ben stood before them breathing and smiling until his teeth went dry it was apparent there were other options available for him if ever they went their separate ways.

Perhaps he'd been considering those options while sitting on the bench with her the past few days, Jackson thought, just as another tram clattered past on Fitzroy Road. For his mind had gone somewhere else, his mystique consigned to the annals of memory. After getting together and sharing their time, ideas and daydreams and everything else their bodies and minds could offer up, where did young couples go next? Though, wherever it was, it didn't look like she and Ben were going to get there together. A self-proclaimed 'club magnet' (just to add to his merchandising status), easily laughing, joking, shouting drinks and dancing, he'd grown suddenly distant and quiet. Emotionally, it was as though he'd dropped into a black hole. He wasn't there. Yes, she had missed something. And the question in her mind now wasn't who he'd been those first few months, but who he was turning into, and why. Hours earlier, after staring out at the bay for what seemed half the afternoon, he delivered his longest spiel in days.

'Queensland, Jack. Picture it. Palm trees swinging in the tropical breeze, the aqua sea and pure white sand.' He scooted closer and surprised her by taking her hand. 'We could be there, you know, after your exams.' His eyes went to the sky as though Queensland was hovering over them. 'Yeah. What a top idea.' He looked at her as if she were a new person, one unrestricted by school commitments and Burger King employment. His voice quickened. 'Listen, I'll meet you at Zep's tonight, around seven, and we can organise it over focaccias and cappuccinos.'

What he used to phrase as questions had become flat statements. He just assumed she'd be where he wanted her to be. Taken in charge again, she nodded. Perhaps she could arrange some time and, if need be, off school too, she allowed herself to think.

The tapping of a stick and the clomping of shoes diverted her. It sounded like a blind man coming down the alley. Alarmed, Jackson shot a glance back up towards Fitzroy Road. The cat was gone, and whoever it was approaching stayed blacked out. Doing her best to put on a brave voice, she asked, 'Are you sure you want to be in this alleyway?'

'Oh. So that's where I am,' replied a deep male voice. The tapping went on for a few more seconds, though, before stopping in front of her, perhaps an arm's length away. She could just make out the shape of a big man with a billed cap and walking stick. Glasses, she thought also, but it took a moment for her to be sure.

He stretched his left hand her way. 'I must have taken a wrong turn. Would you mind directing me back towards the main road?'

'Okay.' Was he partially deaf as well as blind? How could he not hear the traffic out there? Warily, she placed the back of her hand under his heavy palm. She felt a thick ring on his ring finger, and just a nub next to it, before she guided him around to face the road. 'You're right now,' she assured him, retrieving her hand quickly. 'Just walk straight ahead and you'll be out of here.'

'Good. Thanks for that.'

She listened to his tap-tapping going back up the alleyway until another tram clattered past. There was something about the heaviness of that tapping that didn't seem right to her. It was like someone probing for holes in the pavement. There was no scraping noise that a blind man's stick usually makes. Jackson watched the man take shape where the cat had been. He turned right, stepped up on the small kerb and quickly disappeared.

And that's when her gut clenched and her heart thumped hard in her chest. It was the way he took that kerb. Without locating it first with his stick. The stick he lifted in the air like a spear. Trying to calm herself. she froze that picture of him and played it back. Maybe he was just partially blind and knew Fitzroy Road well. Maybe… Her mind spun with conflicting thoughts. If he weren't blind, then why would he be here posing as someone who was?

Staying in touch with the wall. she inched her way further down the alleyway until she came to a corner. Thin light spilled over the ground now. She stretched her head around. About ten metres away, three people sat on crates in the half-lit gloom of a small alcove. One of them was Ben. They faced a small wooden box with a fat candle melted root-like on the top. Two of them were bent forward, elbows on their knees, while Ben remained upright. She watched his dour face as he stared at a spoon being heated over the candle. Across from Ben, a bone-thin figure with a blond ponytail had the pale underside of his right arm extended. A tourniquet was around his elbow and he started slapping the inside of his forearm with the backs of his fingers.

A shaggy-bearded man moved a syringe over that arm.

The thin man balled his hand into a fist and raised his head to the heavens to receive its eternal blessing. Seconds later, the needle penetrated his arm. The plunger pulled back, drawing in a small amount of blood before the mixture was slowly injected.

Jackson turned away, shocked and nauseated, just as a set of yellow lights beamed down the alleyway. A car raced towards her.

'Ben!'

Heads snapped up. The bearded man leapt as if snake-bitten and sprinted away. The addict opened his fist. Gripped in his drug rush, he staggered to his feet, yanked the syringe out of his arm and flicked it like a flower into the night.

Ben was there grabbing her, wild-eyed, and forcing her back into the alcove. 'Here behind the bin! Stay down!' he screamed. 'When they're gone, get away from here!' He snatched his daypack from the wooden box and dashed off.

An old Holden slid into the corner – brakes squealing, tyres howling. It fishtailed, sideswiping the fence, then straightened and picked up speed, streaking past Jackson in a pall of stinking rubber smoke before veering right and catching the addict close up in its lights. Accelerator punched, it went for him, hitting him with a sickening thud and crash of glass. Brake lights flashed as the car swerved sharply, then it roared out of the car park and disappeared.

Jackson stood up trembling. In the renewed darkness, she struggled to collect her senses, to gather up the courage to approach that addict, who had to be lying out there dead. She glanced over at the flickering candle, looking so serenely out of place. A plastic container and a cellophane bag filled with white powder lay beside the box.

People shouted and started running down the alleyway. They'd find the addict. It was up to her what else they'd find. She moved quickly to the box, stuffed the bag in the container and raced off with it tucked like a football in her arm.

2

Man's body found in St Kilda hotel car park

A young man's body was found last night in a car park behind St Kilda's Criterion Hotel. Police say the man – a hit and run victim – carried no identification. Police investigators are appealing to the public for help in determining the identity of the deceased man and the circumstances surrounding his death. The man is described as being in his early 20s, 180 centimetres tall and weighing approximately 65 kilograms. He had long blond hair worn in a ponytail and was wearing faded blue jeans, a grey cotton windcheater and black and white sandshoes. Anyone who can help the police with their investigation is asked to contact Detective Inspector Michael Harris at St Kilda Road Police Headquarters on 9522 9331.

Biting back her anger, Jackson stuffed the article in her pocket and lengthened her stride, mentally scripting what she was going to say to Ben when he opened his door. She'd start with this: 'I'll never forget the roar of that car and the sound of that man being run down.' After that she'd say, 'I've hidden your daypack and that bag of whatever it is (she still couldn't say it) you left behind. So I've done that, okay? But no more. After you reclaim your precious property, you can find yourself another brain-warped girlfriend to accompany you to Queensland, or wherever.'

She arrived at the wrought-iron gate between conjoined units, and went through, following the lane way to the back. Ben's room was there pressed up against a paling fence. Next to the front door was a window covered in heavy curtain. A strip of red light leaked out at the bottom. Stepping closer, she heard lyrics, a tambourine and a guitar.

> And I tell you things aren't quite the same
> Cuz' it makes me feel like I'm a man
> When I put a spike into my vein...

She knocked on the door. There was brief silence inside. Then, as if responding to the knock, another song came on.

She turned the unlocked knob and stepped inside. The red light hit her first, then the blue phosphorescence of the television screen. Sitting opposite it, a metre or so from the doorway, was a dull-eyed boy slumped in an armchair, his cheek resting in the palm of his hand. He wore Mambo shorts, a dark T-shirt and a back-to-front cap over long dreadlocks. Next to his elbow was a cutting board with a syringe and other bits of shooting-up equipment on it. A circus could have paraded through and he wouldn't have registered it.

Next to the CD player, a long-haired Asian sat on the side of a single bed, his head bobbing, his hands beating time to the music. As he showed some signs of life, Jackson moved towards him.

'Do you know where Ben is?' she asked.

His eyes were slow to reach her. 'He's cool.'

Jackson found the player's volume button and turned it so far down she could hear the tap dripping in the sink at the back. 'I'm Ben's girlfriend. I need to know where he is.'

The boy's hands stopped momentarily, though his head didn't. 'Not here.'

Irritation crept into her voice. 'I've worked that much out.' She enunciated her question slowly. 'So-where-is-he-then?'

His head went still. The question seemed to trouble him, as though its answer was submerged too deeply in his mind. Just his cheek muscles moved, twitching slightly, before he found the word. 'Hospital,' he muttered. 'He's cool.'

Jackson stiffened in shock. 'Why, what's wrong with him?'

Stoned, it was too much for his addled brain to deal with. It clamped shut again.

'Tell me!'

The boy's eyes stayed glazed and unblinking. His head bobbed, his fingers patted his thigh. It was just the music he was hearing again.

'At least tell me which hospital he's in!'

Head bobbed, fingers patted.

Jackson turned and raced out the door, along the lane way and out on to the street, where she looked frantically for a phone box. A car swerved past, its driver shouting abuse. Unable to spot a phone, she retreated to the footpath, then sprinted up it in the direction of Fitzroy Road.

Further down the street, a battered HQ Holden started up, turned on its lights and pulled out from the kerb. It moved slowly along the road in the direction of Fitzroy Road. Another car – its headlights flashing low beam to high beam – loomed up and braked at the last second. Passing finally, its angry driver hooted the horn and jerked a two-fingered salute into the air. The Holden's driver and his four passengers took no notice. Their eyes stayed fixed on the road and the girl running up the footpath ahead of them.

3

His battered face stood out like a horror film ad against the ward's soft pastel colours, divider curtains, stacked pillows and crisp sheets. Biting back tears, Jackson sat down next to him. A drip tube was attached to his wrist. His upper lip was stitched lengthwise, and his once-thin brows were so puffy it was impossible to tell whether he was awake or asleep.

'Ben,' she said softly.

He lay there silent and motionless.

A nurse darted in with a clipboard. She greeted Jackson and introduced herself. 'Are you a friend or relative of his?'

'Girlfriend.' As soon as those words were out, she scolded herself. Wanting to learn as much as possible, she should have claimed Ben as her brother. 'He doesn't have any relatives in Melbourne,' she went on in her sweetest voice. 'Can you tell me what happened to him?'

The nurse eyed Ben for a moment. 'I'd say he's been mugged. He's been concussed and has a number of cuts and contusions, as you can see. His ribs are bruised. But the good news is there are no broken bones or internal bleeding. He's fortunate really, when you consider the beating he's taken.' She took up her clipboard again. 'Anyway, he should improve and be out of here in the next few days. When he was admitted last night, he was barely conscious and we couldn't get much out of him. So it's really good you came in.' She smiled pleasantly. 'How did you find out he was here?'

An innocent enough question, but considering where she'd just come from, what was she supposed to say – that some spaced-out druggie, shooting up in her boyfriend's place, told her Ben was in hospital? Jackson glanced over at a big, bearded man propped up against pillows reading a book opposite them. 'One of his friends rang. I don't know which one. Anyway, he just said Ben had been hurt and taken to hospital. So I guessed it was this one.'

After the nurse got Ben's personal details and left, Jackson looked around the ward. In the far corner an emaciated old man was wired up like a power board to monitors that flashed red and green signals like Christmas lights. The bed next to Ben's was curtained off. No sounds or movement came from there. Looking alert and healthy, that big man opposite looked a ring in in this company.

She brought her eyes back to Ben and listened to his troubled breathing. From three storeys down came the growl of city traffic. What activity there was here took place in the corridor where visitors, nurses and mobile patients passed by. There was little to deflect her attention from the gloom, not even a television. She'd have to ring her mum soon and tell her she was leaving Lisa's house in an hour or so, that their exam study had taken more time than they'd expected. If David were still there with her, her mother would croon back something like, 'Yes, dear. That'll be fine. You're a perfect gem for ringing and letting me know.'

What a difference meeting laughing David and his pet Mazda MX5 sports car had made to her. Life was pure joy again, each sweet minute of it. (Well, minus the time all his favourite dish ingredients weren't close at hand, that is.) And it seemed that way for David too, with or without his woolly red neck scarf, patent leather driving gloves and speedway sunnies on. Neither of them was genetically programmed to spend much time out of a 'Significant other's' contact range (to quote chapter four of her Social Psychology text). Both had done so after divorces.

The pain and loneliness of those experiences had them clinging to each other like lottery wins. Jackson wondered why they just didn't live together. Was it because of her? Sometime soon she'd have to sit down with her mum and have a talk about their living arrangements and David.

Ben snorted suddenly. His head tipped to the right and he went quiet again.

Unlike him, at least she had a parent to ring up. Her mind hopped back to the druggies in Ben's room and to the just departed nurse. Had she not come here, the mystery of Ben would have remained. Other than her, and those who did this to him, she doubted anyone else would ever know he'd been here. On the topic of parents, he'd been even less forthcoming than he'd been about his work. 'Gone,' was all he said on the bench one night, shortly after they'd started going out together.

'Gone where?'

'Sally Marie's in Brisbane,' he answered indifferently. 'Samuel Lee's up in tile Kimberleys somewhere, probably hustling pool and a stable of night ladies.'

Sometimes Ben sounded hard to her, as if the suppressed poison of bad experiences had leaked into his voice box. At first this added to his mystique.

'What about brothers or sisters?'

He chuckled dismissively. 'Nah. Sally Marie and Samuel Lee learned from their first mistake in having me.' He put his arm around her, drew her close and concentrated on smoothing up his act. 'Anyway, parents are just a blink in the past, Jack. We are – you and me together – the big, bright future.' He stroked her back and kissed her hair, neck and cheek before their mouths met in the softness of lips and tongues.

She warmed quickly and her heart drummed away for him then.

'If you want to go, I'll tell him you were in to see him when he wakes up.' The big man's voice brought her back to the ward.

She looked over at him.

His book lay flattened under his hands. Large eyes under bushy brows stared placidly over at her. He gave her a friendly smile. 'And if you like, I could tell him when you're planning to come back in again.'

'Thanks. I might just stick around a bit longer. If he doesn't wake up soon, then yes, that'd be good if you could do that.'

The man nodded. 'I suppose the night is just a pup when you're young and living as close to this place as you must be.'

Jackson flinched. That seemed an odd thing for a total stranger to say – well, one as old as him anyway. She gave him a cool glance. 'Yeah, I s'pose.' She dropped her eyes, offering him nothing more.

Moments later, she scolded herself a second time. He was just bored and in the market for some conversation, that was all. Who else could he speak to in here? Nothing to get freaked out about. Tired, upset and now you're going all paranoid as well… Maybe it would be better to leave a message with him, ring back in the morning, then come in after school.

'But when you've got a tram to catch, the night can quickly get beyond a pup,' she said to the man, trying awkwardly to extend his metaphor.

She leaned over Ben and brushed the backs of her fingers over his forehead and cheek. Just as she was about to stand up, the swollen flesh around his eyes began to flicker, and his eyes opened. Jackson watched him struggle to work out where he was. When he moved his head her way, she put on a smile and tried to sound upbeat. 'Got in the way of a truck, did you?'

What she could see of his eyes flicked around briefly before landing back on her. ''ust have,' he laboured to say through thickened lips.

She covered his hand with hers. 'Can you remember what happened?'

'Heading home down a 'ackstreet. Nothing else… Head's sore. Side hur's a lot.'

She told him why, as well as what else the nurse had told her, then added, 'Do you remember if you were carrying much money?'

'No, not 'uch,' he answered vaguely, diverting his eyes from her.

Perhaps it was that, or how quickly he responded that made her suspect he recalled more than he was willing to tell her. She watched his eyes slowly close. 'Well, I've been here a while,' she tested him.

When he didn't answer, she glanced over at the man. 'I s'pose I'd better head home now.' Her breath suddenly choked.

The big man was holding his book up reading again. Seven thick fingers were wrapped around the back of it. On his ring finger was a thick gold ring. The little finger next to it was missing.

Him – the bloke in the alleyway. The shock temporarily paralysed her. Her eyes found the floor; her heart beat hard. So who was he, disguised as a blind man in the alleyway, as a hospital patient now? A policeman, a gang member? Recalling the previous night, Jackson doubted the police connection. They'd never have struck down the addict, surely. So that left one option… Or did it? If he weren't a police plant, then how did he manage to get in that bed?

Visitors' hours were almost over. If she tried to wake Ben up, it would only arouse the man's curiosity. But she couldn't go without warning him! What about leaving a note? Still reading his book over there, the man only had to lift his eyes to read her and what she was doing. What could she do then?

'In hospital for long?' she asked the man, her heart a jackhammer in her chest.

'Long enough to have some tests run on a stomach problem I've had for a while,' he answered in the most casual voice in the hospital.

It *was* the voice in the alleyway; she felt sure of it. 'I hope it's nothing serious,' Jackson lied, thinking the nursing staff would have to know why he was there. So she couldn't ask one of them to give Ben a note. In desperation, she struck on an idea.

She stood up. 'Have to go. As soon as I find my train ticket, that is,' she said in a voice meant to carry. She placed her school bag on the bed and opened it up. 'Hopefully it's in here.' She took out her books and stacked them precariously on the bedside table, then foraged through her bag knowing exactly where her train ticket was. She nudged the top book with her elbow, causing it to fall on the bed. 'Oh, here it is.' She stuffed an old sales docket in her pocket, gathered up what was on the table and shoved it back in her bag, mindful of stowing a blank exercise book and biro at the top.

Flashing her warmest fake smile at the man, she headed for the door. 'Goodbye.'

'Back in tomorrow then?'

'Or the next day maybe,' she answered, faking a yawn. She patted her bag. 'I'll just have to see how the homework is going.'

The big man nodded his understanding.

Down the corridor Jackson found a public phone and rang her mother. 'Hi, Mum. I thought I'd better ring. Lisa bought a new Jack

Johnson CD today, so we've been slow getting into the books.' A wave of skin tingling discomfort hit her – the price of lying. But what else could she say?'I should be home by eleven. Is that all right?'

'Yes, of course, dear. I'm pleased you rang. There's a bowl of strawberries in the fridge for you when you get home.'

David had to be there.

'Thanks, Mum. You're a beauty.' After hanging up, she plopped down in a chair and grabbed the exercise book and biro from her bag, and began writing.

> Ben – BE CAREFUL!
>
> I've got what you left behind after sale time last night, and I'm scared. I've thought about throwing it in the ocean. I know this will sound crazy, but I'm certain the big man in the bed across from you was in the car that killed the man in the car park last night. So even if you start to feel better, don't say so. Pretend to be friendly, because he will; or just pretend you're sleeping. I'll be back in again after school tomorrow, okay? It'll be a stage performance – all smiles and loud greetings. But when we talk it'll be low because we've got to work out what to do, and fast!
>
> See you tomorrow,
> Jack

She tore the note out and folded it up in a tiny square. Enclosing it in her fist, she returned to the ward. 'Oh, there it is,' she called out, looking at the book on Ben's bed. As she picked it up in her left hand, she pulled Ben's blanket down with her right and ran the tips of her fingers down his forearm until she felt his name band. She wedged the note inside it. It was the best she could do. 'Goodbye again,' she said in a jaunty voice.

'Goodbye.'

Outside, the street was shiny with rain. Jackson put her bag over her shoulder and started walking quickly towards the city centre, anxious to get home.

Arriving at Spencer Street station, she turned to descend the steps when a youth in oversized clothes pressed in on her right. She veered away and bumped into another youth with a shaved head. Someone brushed up behind her. Panic-stricken, she raced down the steps.

Others joined in and stayed close behind, their laughter ringing in her ears.

'Keep her movin', movin', movin',' one sang out, enjoying himself.

'Heard that on the telly once.'

'She's got the legs of a racehorse.'

'Olympic finals don't come quicker than this.'

At the bottom, a beak-faced man with long red hair and a spindly goatee stepped out from around a corner, arms outspread, blocking her way. They all crowded in on her, pressing her against the wall.

Before she could scream, the beak-faced man leaned in close. 'Ward 5A,' he said calmly. 'First bed on the right, isn't it? Come with us quietly now or your boyfriend's next stop's the morgue.'

Passers-by: they had to know what was happening. They had to sense her terror. Why couldn't they meet her eyes and report what they saw? But it was as though they'd been whipped across the face. They just wouldn't look around; they just didn't want to know.

When commuter numbers thinned out, she was jostled towards a green door with a sign saying, STAFF ONLY. Bundled inside the small room, she was pinned against a cleaning locker.

The beak-faced man stepped up, just centimetres away, and gave her a grin like a shark's. 'Nick's the name, pleasure's the game.' With that, he glanced over his shoulder seeking the plaudits of those around him.'And you are?' he rasped, his eyes on her again.

'Jackson. Why are you doing this?'

'Jackson,' he repeated. 'Love the name.' He ran his eyes down her. 'To answer your question, Jackson, we've gotta problem with your dickhead boyfriend and the number of times he's been doing business on turf not his own.'

'Only the once. And it was obviously a mistake. I'm sure he knows that now.'

'Only once, you say?' His smile widened. 'We are talking about Ben Ekin? St Kilda dog-box resident, Brad Pitt lookalike, with a small gold earring to complement his equally small brain?'

When she didn't respond, he answered for her, 'Yes, him. Take my word for it, more than once. And if he's allowed to continue, well then, every bastard and his mongrel dog as the story goes.' He glanced over at two others busily doing something beside him.

'He's in hospital because of it. The lesson's been learned, surely.' Her body wasn't cooperating. Tears sprang up. Breathing got difficult.

Nick jerked his head her way again. 'Maybe. But he still owes us. His car park rental fee is long overdue.'

On the blurred edge of her vision she saw the two beside Nick move to the basin next to her. One held a small square of folded paper, the other a syringe and a vial.

Nick kept talking. 'When we tried to…'

Numb with fear, she only caught snippets of what he was saying.

'…he had trouble giving us the right answers…'

Water from the tap half-filled the vial.

'… Maybe he got too stressed too early…'

The paper was unfolded.

'…threw a punch…'

White powder was tipped into the vial.

'…lost consciousness… '

Stirred, the powder dissolved.

'… So who should we see later streaking up the street to…'

The boy moved in, a belt dangling from his hand.

'… The powder freak in his dog-box proved helpful. "Hospital," he just managed to croak, during a needle and musical interlude. Just that single word, but enough. So now, Jackson, it's your turn to be helpful.'

Her horror heightened as the boy wrapped the belt around her arm, just above the elbow. He pulled it tight, then took out a cooking spoon and a cigarette lighter.

'Please don't do this,' she pleaded, trying to wrench her arms free.

'Ssshh. Ward 5A. The first bed on the right, remember?' Nick turned to his accomplice, who was heating the spoon's contents. 'Eight grams, right?'

'Not a milligram less.'

Satisfied, Nick grabbed her hand and lifted it up. 'Check out the stick she calls an arm. I've seen more meat on a butcher's apron.' Playing to his audience, he took the syringe, dropped his jaw and ogled it at eye level. 'Mmm.' He scratched the top of his head like a mad scientist. 'A change of needles might be called for, Boris. This one could go in and come out the other side.' From amongst the sniggering faces, his closed in again on hers. 'Remind you of a science class at school? It does me.'

The spoon was placed on the side of the sink. The needle probed its contents. The plunger was pulled back, drawing the solution up into the syringe.

'Please,' she blubbered, on the edge of hysteria. 'This makes no sense. What do you want from me?'

Still in actor's mode, Nick's jaw dropped, his eyes went huge in mock-amazement. 'What do we want? Is that what I heard?'

She nodded like a little girl.

'What a superb question. The possibilities are endless.' Pulling back a little, he rubbed his hand over her breasts, then down her stomach. The hand paused as he glared hard-eyed and indicated the syringe being held next to her. 'What you see there is twice the four grams that constitutes a person's first hit-up of smack. Called the Beginners' Course, it is. But you, having such a true believer boyfriend, will be good for twice that amount, now won't you?'

That animal grin beat down on her.

The plunger was nudged down. White liquid seeped out the needle.

Nick took the syringe and ran the needle over the inside of Jackson's forearm, tracing her veins. 'Where'd you find the syringe?' he asked the man at the basin.

'Just off Fitzroy Road, in a rubbish bin next to the mini-market. Lots to choose from there.'

'Always are.' The needle prodded Jackson's skin without penetrating. 'You wore your gloves, didn't you?'

'The thick ones. It'd be a death sentence not to.'

'Yes… One thing about feeling tension,' Nick said, turning his attention back to Jackson. 'It makes the veins in your arm stick out. Never a problem finding a target.'

Her eyes begged, but words just wouldn't come out.

'Now tell us, Jackson, where lies the boyfriend's stash of smack?'

4

Barrelling through the front door the next evening, Jackson bumped shoulders with her mother standing in front of the full-length mirror modelling her new blonde-highlighted hair, low-cut purple pantsuit and Italian sandals. 'Sorry, Mum.'

'You're late again, dear,' her mother commented, her Yves Saint Laurent eau de toilette wafting like a fresh coat of paint through the hallway. The mirror claimed her attention again. She eyed it appraisingly, then leaned forward with tweezers and plucked a wayward hair from her eyebrow. 'More study to do?'

'Yes, Mum.' Though the study of Island Air flights to Flinders Island, passenger screening procedures at Moorabin Airport, Chicken Feed wedding bands and St Vinnie's swallowed-a-bowling-ball maternity dresses obviously weren't what her mother was referring to.

'Anyway, dear, David and I are going out for an early tea and late film,' she said, brightening up. Having passed the mirror test, and boasting a satisfied smile, she turned to her daughter and suddenly scowled. 'Are you sure you're eating all right? You've been looking very tired and worn the past couple of days.'

'I'm fine, Mum,' Jackson lied again, still feeling jittery after the train station horror. 'There's just a lot of pressure on at school at the moment, that's all.'

Her mind flicked back through the afternoon spent at the hospital, the airport and back in the city. Though she'd just got home, she knew now was the best time to ask her mother about going away, mind-numbing as that thought was. 'Mum, classes finished today. Exams start in nine days' time.' Her voice sounded distant, disembodied. 'I was wondering if

30

I could go over to Flinders, check in with Aunt Louise at the hotel and use the shack for some concentrated study time.'

'Can you get the time off work?'

'Yes, no worries.' Wrong, there was that worry, but she'd have to quit Burger King if they didn't give it to her.

Headlights shone through the window briefly as David's sports car swept into the driveway, revving away its presence. Two sets of two quick door knocks would soon follow.

Her mother reached into her purse and handed Jackson her credit card. 'Use this to make the booking. I'll give you a hundred dollars towards it. The rest you'll have to pay back. We'll talk about the details later.' She planted a kiss on her daughter's cheek. 'Love you.'

The knocks came just as she opened the door. She positioned her pink night glasses as though her eyes were on top of her head, spread her arms out wide and threw her head back in a 'take-all-of-me' pose. 'I ask you, David. Are you up to this?'

He beamed his fridge magnet smile and laughed, predictably. 'Next to you, my heart, Nicole Kidman's the bag lady at the fish and chip shop.'

Delighted with life, they kissed quickly and left.

Jackson turned and looked at her 'very tired and worn' self in the mirror. She agreed with her mother. Her school jeans, blouse and jumper were overdue for the washing machine. Her long, black corkscrew hair looked drier and shaggier than ever; her face was tight with strain; her dark eyes glazed with fatigue. Only if she'd been the adopted daughter of an Asian or African family would she have contrasted with her fair-skinned parents more. Well, her mother anyway. Her father might have darkened up since she'd last seen him. He'd found someone in Sydney four years ago who he could have a natural family with, and she hadn't laid eyes on him since, though he sent her Christmas and birthday presents and always rang around New Years. On the responsibility ladder, he was at least a rung or two up from Ben's father.

Having seen too much of herself, and intent on getting her mind back to the present, she turned and moved down the hallway to her room.

Rummaging through her school bag, she took out a writing pad, a map of the Bass Strait Islands and a biro and dropped them on her bed. Time was suddenly important. There was so much to do. But in the deep quiet of her room, Spencer Street station, Nick's voice and grin and that wandering needle started filling her mind again. She slumped down on the bed and dropped her head in her hands.

Pinned against that locker, everything she could feel was focused on that needle. At what point would it break the skin? Her heart drummed away, her nose and eyes ran. Her terror-struck voice whimpered in her ears, 'I don't know where it is, but…but I'll ask,' she sputtered, dumb with fear. 'For sure, I'll ask him when he's right! I promise I will!'

That same shark's grin bore down on her. 'When he's right, you say. And when do you reckon that'll be?'

Her terror waned, ever so slightly. 'Five or six days.'

Just her nose sniffling away, otherwise tense silence. That needle didn't move.

Nick grinned that grin and looked around at his audience. 'I feel a human moment coming on.'

On cue, his minions grinned back, all shiny-eyed.

He glared at her. 'Three days, seventy-two hours. Not a minute more. Today is Thursday and the time is…'

'Ten past nine, Nick,' the minion on his left noted.

'Right. We'll meet at the boyfriend's room then on Sunday, ten past nine. You'll be there waiting eagerly for us, won't you?'

'Yes,' her voice quivered. Beaten down, a rush of emotion hit her. Her throat tightened. She sobbed, her eyes spilling tears.

Nick shook his head in mock despair. 'Dear oh dear oh dear.' He glanced to his left. 'Get something to mop her face with, will you? We'll be floating in it before long.'

Seconds later a wad of toilet paper appeared and rubbed at her cheeks, roughly pinching her nose, before being tossed in the basin.

'Ears wide open now?'

She nodded.

'Then listen up.' Nick leant close again, his gluey eyes all over her. 'We'll

want to know precisely where the heroin is, and you'll go with us to get it, won't! you?'

Her responses were automatic. 'Yes.'

'Excellent.'

The needle lifted slowly. Everything else came after that.

'Know that if you or anyone else go to the boys in blue, we'll know. And sadly, if you do, the debt will still be owed and I'll have to arrange for some other form of payment.' He shrugged and extended his hands palms up. 'I mean, if boyfriend Ben suddenly turned up shiny coffin-bound, whose fault would that be?'

'Mine.'

He sighed as if disappointed. 'I'm afraid so.' He handed the syringe back to the man who'd prepared it, then slid his tongue slowly along his upper lip and placed his hand inside her thigh. He moved it to her crotch and kept it there, all the time ogling her with that grin. 'Sunday night then, Jackson. And if you've done what needs to be done, there'll be no reason for us to get this close again…if you've done what needs to be done.' He turned and strolled towards the door, the others falling in line behind him.

Once they'd gone, she went to the door and stared out at the normalcy of train station life. A man brushed past eyeing her strangely.

She eyed him back. People were prepared to see her again.

'Bastards,' she whimpered now, still clinging to her anger and humiliation.

Turning, she noticed the curtain over her window was partially opened. She went over and peeked out, thinking. Besides knowing her first name and that Ben was her boyfriend, what else did they know? That information she gave to the hospital nurse, the big man would have listened to. He could have passed it on. The crucial thing was, did they know her address? *'…when you're young and living as close to this place as you must be.'* Well, the big man obviously didn't. And after jumping in and out of trains and taking more than two hours to get home, she was certain she'd not been followed by any of them. No, they couldn't know, she decided.

So wouldn't it just be easier to give that sleazebag Nick what he was after? But the problem with that centred on what Ben mumbled to her at the hospital earlier that afternoon.

'I read your note,' he said, looking desperate.

She glanced at his wrist and noticed it was no longer under his band.

'Jack, you've gotta hide what you found.'

No more illusions, she decided. Her eyes drilled him. 'The heroin, you mean?' Her tone was hard, accusing.

He winced as if the word hurt him. 'If it's lost, I'm dog's meat. I'll ex'lain e'erything when I'm outta here. 'romise.'

That'll be a first, she thought, before her eyes followed his across the ward. She issued her second greeting smile to their reason for having to mumble. As the big man's eyes were on his book again, he didn't acknowledge it. He had to be Australia's slowest reader. In the ten minutes she'd been there, she hadn't heard or seen him turn a page, and he wasn't the sort of man who would do that delicately. She looked down at Ben again, feeling her stomach twisting, her life rocketing out of control, and stuck another note in his hand.

Ben —

Read this while I smile occasionally at that pig in the bed opposite and say things loudly for his benefit. The gang that attacked you got a hold of me last night. They told me they'd do things to me if I didn't tell them where the heroin (why didn't you tell me?) supply was. I convinced them that I didn't know, but that you did. I had no choice, Ben. If wasn't nice what they were doing. They're such rat meat. Anyway, they've given me three days to get the information from you. I'm supposed to meet them at your room on Sunday night.

When his stunned eyes looked back up at her, she whispered, 'I need to think.' Then she raised her voice and went into actor's mode. 'Gotta go now. I'll be back tonight, okay?' She bent down and kissed his forehead.

Last night's train station terror hit her again. The smirks on their faces and that rubbish-bin needle. Her eyes and nose streaming tears and gunk, and that sleazebag's hands all over her. So give him what he wanted after what he and his mongrel friends did to her? Bitter tears welled up again. 'No,' she muttered to herself. 'No way.' There was enough anger, stubbornness and pride in her now to do this, if she and Ben could get away, get lost, so they could talk about everything that was happening to them: their dying relationship, him lying to her and his heroin temporarily hidden under firewood in the backyard.

She got on the Internet and made a booking with Island Air, then she sat down and began writing.

Ben –

Last note. You and I NEED to talk somewhere far away from here. Pretend this is a map of Queensland and we're looking at it and talking about places there we want to visit, so that he'll think that's where we're going. Now read on. This is really a map of Flinders Island. That's where I'll be, not Queensland. I have an aunt who works at the hotel in Whitemark. You MUST get out of the hospital BEFORE SUNDAY NIGHT and fly Island Air from Moorabin Airport down to Flinders Island and the Whitemark Hotel without anyone knowing. That won't be easy, because you're being watched and you'll be followed. Somehow you'll have to lose them. Maybe use a disguise, I don't know. But I just can't think of any other option, other than things getting even worse for you. Be really careful Ben and GET TO THE WHITEMARK HOTEL.

She crammed everything back into her bag and left for the hospital.

5

She sat alone in the Whitemark Hotel lounge bar shuddering from the trauma of recent memory. For someone who'd never felt the power of stupefying fear before being bailed up in a Spencer Street station cleaning room, she considered herself a veteran of the emotion now. Who else her age, and in such a short period of time, had witnessed a druggie being run down at close quarters? Had watched a heroin-filled syringe and dirty needle come within a hair's breadth of puncturing their skin while being pinned to a sink? Or, as a brain-dead heroin transporter, had run the gauntlet of metal detectors and airport staff at Moorabin Airport? It was that most recent terrifying experience she dwelled on now. At least suicide bombers, with their Koran, detonators and bags of explosives strapped to their bodies, were convinced they were going to a better world after earthly oblivion. Wearing her maternity dress over a pregnancy swell of heroin and bubble wrap, and with that imitation wedding band on her finger, there were no such 'better world' assurances for her if she'd been prevented from boarding that plane. Just another sort of earthly oblivion: unimaginable humiliation, a criminal record and designated uni time spent in prison, or at best, on community service orders.

The images and her emotions from the previous day came flooding back.

Panic rose in her chest, turning her legs limp, and all that earlier anger and stubbornness evaporated as she approached Moorabin's departure door officialdom. But it was too late to turn around. How could she when she was always in their sight as the plane's third and final passenger? Fortunately, she didn't have to say anything. Blank with terror (caught in Indonesia, she'd be shot; in Singapore, hanged), barely able to breathe, she doubted she retained the language sense to form sentences. Her concentration – such as it was – focused on keeping her hands steady while she showed her ticket, handed over her bag for inspection and prayed.

Smiled at, wished a pleasant journey and waved through within seconds, the heat of fear didn't ease until she arrived at Flinders, ducked into the airport toilet to unload and change, then caught a ride the short distance into Whitemark.

She breathed a heavy sigh and looked down at the table, as smooth and shiny as a new coffin. Her stomach turned again recalling where and when she last heard that word used.

To divert her mind, she extended her fingers and concentrated on spreading drops of fallen condensation from her Coke can over the table that could double as a mirror. It seemed out of place here. For there was little else inside this old, two-storey hotel or, for that matter, outside in the faded buildings, rusted hulks of cars, or in the time-worn clothes of the occasional passers-by that could begin to match the table's sheen.

She hadn't experienced such quiet since the last time she was here with her mother. She'd thought then that there couldn't have been another town in all Australia more divorced from big city life than this place. No signs, billboards, neon messages to read. Three years on and they still hadn't arrived. Having someone enter your field of vision here was an event. And at dusk, when the setting sun streaked the sky gold, pink and purple, it seemed she was the only person in the visible world to witness it.

She swigged away on her Coke, looking at her closed books and catching snatches of conversation and gruff laughter from the front bar. Her eyes wandered. On the wall opposite the counter were ageing photos of the century-old hotel, a large football team ladder and a sign that read,

ENSURE BRAIN
IS ENGAGED
BEFORE PUTTING
MOUTH INTO GEAR.

Further along the wall hung a large wooden map of the island, shaped like a crayfish. A few wavering lines indicated roads. Besides Whitcmark – scrolled in block letters over half the map – there were little places like Northeast River on the island's northern tip, Palana, Killiecrankie and Wyabelena on the west coast, and Lady Barron in the south.

Nothing featured along the east coast, though, where her mother and father still shared ownership of their Bushed Out retreat – a flat-roofed, two-room shack surrounded by bush and native trees.

Minutes later an older man with tangled white hair, a frothy beard and wearing a frayed jumper and jeans strode through the door and sat down on a stool at the counter.

Aunt Louise came in from the front bar and glanced over at her. 'How's the study going?' she called out.

'Great.'

'Uh huh.' She wasn't convinced. 'I'll be over in a sec.' She turned towards the man. 'Can I help you?' she asked, not appearing to know him.

The man ordered a small beer in a small voice. Unusual for this place, Jackson thought, before fingering another droplet off her Coke can. If Ben didn't get here by tomorrow, she'd leave him a note, then buy some food and head off for the shack, where hopefully she could coax her mind to do some studying. Though there was the small problem of how to get out there.

Her aunt escaped the bar momentarily and sat down opposite her. 'How'd you sleep?'

With my bag hidden under the bed, Jackson answered in her mind. She forced a smile. 'Fine, thanks.'

'Good.'

Five years younger than her brother – Jackson's Christmas and birthday-only father, Geoff – Louise had come here on a working holiday twenty years ago and met and married solitary Tom, a grazier fifteen years her senior. According to mother Margaret, she decided to have a quick child by him before his sperm count disappeared, along with the rest of him. Though, from seeing them together, it was apparent there was more to their relationship than that. When their daughter, Tess, started studying psychology at Sydney Uni, while living with a boyfriend up there and seeing more of her Uncle Geoff than Jackson had ever seen of him, Aunt Louise started working at the hotel to help pay her daughter's expenses.

'I must admit,' Louise went on now, 'I was surprised to get your phone call yesterday. A day and half is fairly short notice.' She leaned closer. 'Everything all right on the home front?'

Not really. 'Yes, terrific.' These past few days Jackson had learned how to smile when she really wanted to hide, to put on a cheerful voice when she really felt like shrieking. 'It's just that exams are going to make a lot of difference to what I do next year.' The same could also be said for the heroin under the bed upstairs. 'I just couldn't settle into study mode at home, so I thought I'd try here.'

'Well, don't go all solitary on me out there. Wholesome meals and regular de-briefings at my place will be just as important as concentrated study for top exam performances.'

'Oy, the lovely Louise!' someone shouted from the front bar.

'Where's she napping?' A whistle pierced the air. 'Tongues are turning to dust in here!'

'Right, I'm about to mount the rescue effort!' Louise shouted back, before eyeing Jackson again. 'My shift finishes at five. If you want to wait around town, I can give you a lift to the shack then.'

Jackson nodded. 'Thanks.'

Her aunt would most likely want to stick around once she did that, making a pot of tea, insisting on helping her unpack, then inviting her back to her place for an exam-strengthening meal cooked and served by quiet, but friendly-enough Tom. That is, if she hadn't spotted the real reason for Jackson being here first. Bowman's was across the road from the hotel. There'd be no Thredbo Mountain Bike Classic winners amongst his lot of rental bikes. But they were capable of getting her to Bushed Out if she had the legs for it.

'Actually, I might just see how I go, okay?'

'Okay.' Louise got up and returned the front bar to an accompaniment of polite applause.

Jackson glanced back over at the man on the stool. He'd barely touched his beer. She angled her head around and got a better view of him: the sunken cheeks, leathery skin, bowed shoulders. He stared at that football ladder as if he were about to sit his own exam on it. In his fifties, she reckoned. Probably some hermit down on his luck, living in a dog box (Nick's close words again) with his mind locked on the events that got him there, like in that Henry Lawson short story she'd read in school recently.

Perhaps she should go change her clothes and take another walk to get her legs fit if she decided to bike across to the shack. But she hesitated. She hadn't talked to anyone but her aunt since she'd arrived. For that reason, she thought she shared something with that solitary man at the bar. 'Do you live in Whitemark?' she asked him softly.

'Uh?' It was as though someone had cracked a whip. He turned round. 'Sorry.'

She repeated the question.

'Not in Whitemark, no.'

Jackson took note of his awkwardness. It wasn't surprising, him being what he was and all. 'I was just looking at that map up there and thinking how old it must be,' she said.

The man's eyes followed hers.

'It shows the road that goes across to the east coast,' she continued, 'but nothing at the end of it.'

'There's not much there. Just sand and ocean and scrubby trees. Last exit to nowhere, really. Sleep a hundred years out there, wake up and nothing would've changed.'

Jackson had to strain to hear him. 'So do you know what condition the road's in now?'

'Good, until you get to the last bit, the dirt road section. Then it gets a bit lumpy.'

The road hadn't changed much, then. She warmed to the man, and other questions entered her head, like why he knew so much about the Patriarch area. But she decided not to ask them. Bowman would be good for an answer or two, she decided, if Ben and his driver's licence didn't show up soon.

'It was good talking to you,' she said, getting up. 'I might just see what's going on outside. It's a lovely day for a walk, don't you think?' she said, choosing her oldies-friendly words carefully.

'It is, yes,' he answered, watching her leave. Pete sipped his beer, and it struck him that with the exception of the grazier he leased his shack from, and his son, he hadn't talked so much to anyone since he'd arrived on the island. He sat there and thought about that.

'Another beer?'

It was as though the bar lady had descended from the roof.

'No, thanks,' Pete answered, shaking his head. 'Any more and I'll be camping here the night.'

'It's been done before.' Louise waited for a reply but didn't get one. 'Mind the traffic then,' she said, taking the empty glass and returning to the front bar.

Pete left the hotel, got into his old VW Beetle and drove most of the way back to Patriarch Inlet before realising he'd forgotten to buy his monthly supply of food and beer and a new shovel. He turned round and headed back to town.

6

At first Jackson felt euphoric, despite her worries. The breeze was at her back. There were the sweet smells of pine trees and freshly cut hay. And the only sounds came from the hum of her bicycle wheels on the road and the echoing cries of magpies perched on fence posts.

Soon the road began to wind and rise. Working hard in the lowest gear, she quickly grew leg-weary. She started asking herself why she was carrying that bag of powder all the way over to the other side when there was so much empty space close by. There were Jogs and earth mounds she could use to step over the barbed wire fencing. Rocks were scattered next to trees in the paddocks. She could put the bag of powder in her daypack, mark a tree in some way and use rocks to cover it up. But just when she'd locate a likely site, a distant farmhouse crept into view, or occasional vehicles passed by. A moving figure in those paddocks would easily be spotted and be certain to arouse suspicion. So, despite the fatigue that came from pushing her supply-heavy bike up the steep road, if what surrounded her now was considered somewhere by that old man, then it was far better to push on and get to the shack, his version of nowhere.

Finally over the top, the road dipped and she started free wheeling down. But that soon challenged her as well, as the road deteriorated the further she went. Soon the smells of farmland and trees were replaced by the stench of maggot-infested roadkill rotting on the road. She imagined this road at night, thick with animals sitting up, their eyes reflecting yellow coins in the beams of oncoming headlights. Though the only live animals she could lay her eyes on now – when she dared look up – were the stilled shapes of a few sheep and cattle blurred by the sun.

The road straightened and flattened finally. Bitumen gave way to dirt, which softened under a thickening layer of sand. The same wasted stone cottages and roofless sheds, rusted-out windmills and water tanks she remembered from her last visit, sat abandoned on the hard, bleached paddocks.

The wind swung around and blew grit in her face. Her eyes stung and watered. Stops became more frequent. Bent over along the side of the road, it took more and more time for her to recover and continue. When she did get back on her bike, she pedalled harder, but moved no faster in a stiffening wind that slapped her clothes like small flags.

A welcoming strip of green finally showed on the horizon. The road led into bush, but pedalling didn't get any easier. Sand built up and the road got bumpy with the many shallow roots that ran across it. Around each corner she expected to see the turn-off and the Bushed Out sign on the gate. But there was only more road getting softer and rougher and narrower, making it more and more difficult to control her top-heavy bike.

The bush thickened, the wind hissed. Bark and twigs flew across the road. Branches lashed the air and other branches like whips, closer and closer to her.

Bushed Out had to be close. It wouldn't be long, she kept telling herself.

A rumbling noise swept over, jarring her tight nerves. Images of the shack vanished as she tried to work out what the sound was. Trees, or waves crashing out on the coast? It came from behind her, though. So it couldn't be the ocean. The sound lapsed in a renewed rush of wind. A thought, born of fear, struck her. Maybe the sound was the ocean. Maybe she'd taken a wrong turn and was just biking around in some great circle. How could she know? Don't panic, she cautioned herself after she had. The road went back as well as forward. She had food and water. All she had to do was turn around to get out of the trees and back on to that open road. The wind, so anxious to push her away now, would work for her then.

She'd give it another ten minutes, no more. And that thought comforted her as she went round another bend and descended roughly, gathering speed. That rumbling sounded again, closer. A car engine, she realised, just as another tree root showed in the middle of the road. She veered left. The root moved with her. 'Snake!' she screamed. She braked hard, the bike skidding over the black snake's tail. It reared up. Her bike lurched and she was suddenly airborne, the ground and that snake rushing up at her, the sound of her screaming ringing in her ears.

7

It had been a rough flight and it got rougher as the plane banked sharply to the left.

'You might want to wrap those seat belts around you a second time,' the pilot shouted out over the drone of the engines. 'And while you're considering the need to do that, I'll just skirt around this bit of turbulence. Then things should settle down.'

Nick trusted the pilot was using his headset for second opinions and not for rant and roll, as he was doing. Feeling suddenly queasy, he switched off The Spazzys' *Aloha! Go Bananas* and glanced out the window, where cloud filled the sky like milk filling a bowl. Moments later the rodeo ride ended, at least temporarily.

This was hardly the soft-pillow flight he'd got to lush Lord Howe Island a couple of years back. Though Flinders wasn't an enforced holiday like Lord Howe had been. With any luck at all, he'd be on the next plane off the island bound for Melbourne. Then where would he go? Now that was what kept his mind in a swirl, and had ever since Copper Harris – legendary lip-reader and bionic ear hearing specialist – passed along Jackson's note to boyfriend Ben.

Of course Harris and company trusted he'd be back. But what say he let out a quiet word on St Kilda streets about a smack supply going for a rock-bottom price. He knew the ones to contact. The same ones he got to track Jackson on the three trams, the train and a taxi out to Moorabin. That St Kilda sniffer squad could hire themselves out as tracker dogs, seeing as they did the same thing with the boyfriend. They'd put the stoppers on him, though, for an agreed-upon price: five times greater, sadly, than the squad's spot-the-Flinders-Island-smack-runner effort.

Hadn't shed their talent for realising a profit, had they? Classic working man's approach: over-award wages and low running costs. For example, there wasn't a packet being spent on the boyfriend's room and board at the moment. A locked, windowless basement, together with limited sustenance – a daily Big Mac, fries and Coke, and a half a gram needle fix that wasn't enough to anaesthetise a cockroach – can do strange things to budding smackheads. They become…what's the word? Pliable. Yeah, that's it, pliable in the god-forsaken gloom. As a much-photographed trump card, the boyfriend's cell time guaranteed that Nick would be leaving Flinders with what he'd come for. Transaction completed, pliable Ben might even be offered an opportunity to run a chore or two for the White Dragons, in exchange for the light of day. Not that Nick necessarily planned to be there when that happened.

'Am I good or what?' he mumbled to himself, a satisfied grin on his face. 'Sharp as a razor blade, subtle as a moonbeam.' Indeed, he could turn his eager hand to most anything. Well, he had, starting in school, and got top marks all the way through as well, didn't he? He had a talent that preserved his place in the system when others, with similar interests and outside working hours, were regularly given their early release papers. At school, when informed of an associate's imminent departure, he'd shake his head and open his palms to the heavens at the inevitability of expulsion for such A1 dickheads who refused to toe the school line. 'After all,' he often said to teaching staff then, 'school is a training ground for society, is it not?' It certainly had been for him. And like society, schools could not allow such reprobates to continually undo all the good work that was going on inside their inviolable chambers of learning. 'Ooooeee,' he muttered, 'still a walking, talking dictionary, are you not, number one?' Anyhow, it was best to get rid of the knuckle-draggers; make them find their own way in the big-dog-eat-small-dog world of ours, to quote his mentor, Copper Harris.

Through a break in the clouds he looked down at the sea, a mass of white caps like maggots swarming into a wound.

'Flinders on the horizon,' the pilot called out. 'Should have you steady on the ground in ten minutes.'

Actually, he'd thought about going through to the heady heights of grade twelve; he seriously had. His teachers and the principal encouraged him to. But that was before he was offered the chance to make it big in the powder trade. An opportunity that only came along 'once in a lifetime for those with an enterprising bent', a well-disguised Copper Harris explained to him and two other prospective White Dragons, of Asian persuasion, one night in a Footscray alleyway. Not the most original line of sales pitch he'd ever heard. But then, this wasn't the first time he'd listened to the detective inspector's lecture on the 'value of multicultural cooperation in achieving mutually beneficial outcomes'. No, certainly not. In his role as life coach, Harris had been a regular visitor to his high school as the Police Department's Anti-drug Spokesperson for the South-eastern Suburbs. Big title. Big, versatile man. So in grades nine and ten, Nick had listened carefully to him, watched his videos and calculated all those bar graph statistics on the whiteboard. Anyone who had the good copper's contacts deserved to be listened to.

The plane started to descend.

He still owed his St Kilda associates for services rendered on the pair in question, didn't he? Plus there'd be a muffler, a guide dog owner's, an Alzheimer's, a call it-what-you-like fee for saying nothing, seeing nothing and knowing nothing about him and his smack sale.

After retrieving the supply from the local hotel down there, he'd have to drop its price on the Saintland market, *if* he decided to quick sell and detour west with a new wardrobe, haircut and shave, and up-to-date passport as a special precaution. Pity about his tattoos. Still, he could get them removed when he got over there. The option was Copper Harris's seventy-five per cent against the paltry twenty-five per cent doled out to the White Dragons, lots of them. Not much to fill his own pocket after all the effort he'd put into this one.

Besides, he'd served his long apprenticeship with distinction, hadn't he? It was time to branch out – a long way out – and test the powder trade market in a less competitive environment. To do that, he'd worked out, required a six-figure sum. With seventy-five per cent of the discounted quarter of a million dollar St Kilda sale warming *his* pocket, instead of Harris's, it would be all systems go in implementing his own first-ever, personal business plan. No high-risk operation either, if he could get in and out quickly here. Go to the hotel. Find Jackson. Hand over the boyfriend's letter – written in chook-track English while being dictated to him by others – appealing to her to take full advantage of the Flinders one-off smack courier service. As proof positive that the boyfriend wouldn't be joining her on their island escapade, Nick would exhibit Ben's gold watch and the recent photo of him with a syringe hanging out of his vein. He'd explain to her, if need be, that big-haul smack merchants average about ten years in the lock-up if she should decide to involve officialdom in the equation.

One-way street, really. After being presented with the supply in question, he'd make enquiries about her future; whether she'd like to meet a White Dragon or two for a regular squeeze in the back of the Holden. If not, he'd recommend that she have a chat with her beefwit boyfriend about the benefits of a quiet return to Melbourne streets, or a visit to tropical Queensland, with a mind to entering into gainful employment and, perhaps, enrolling in a methadone substitution program. Solid options for his future: non-threatening and harassment-free. As well, it required so little to do or remember, just sensible restraint and a locked mouth.

His seat dropped suddenly with the rest of the plane. Geez, his gut wasn't enjoying this. If ever he decided to pilot aircraft, he'd have to keep a bucket between his legs. As they turned sharply over the narrow strip of coast and a small town with small houses, his stomach pushed up towards his throat. He concentrated hard on the spinnakers of cloud shadow that chased each other across the paddocks and up the rugged hills below.

The plane flattened and started its approach towards a landing strip that ended just metres from the shoreline. You wouldn't want to overshoot it unless you dropped the plane's wheels for pontoons, he speculated, before forcing his thoughts back to the world of business. Yes, he'd done the right thing in not having the girlfriend escorted back from Moorabin, as the others had so eagerly suggested.

Just one lingering problem, though: how best to settle in under that big western sky without having the good copper knocking on his door. No problems with the White Dragons: grunters and thumpers, the lot of them. Average at maths, but not worth a sparrow's fart in geography. Had difficulty working out how to get to the other side of a traffic circle. No, no hassles there. But Copper Harris was a very different proposition. Had a reputation that trailed him like a comet's tail. While admittedly not a bright spark for sales pitches, he was tenacious – like a pit bull after a new bone. A couple of blokes Nick had heard about – over the White Dragon chat-line-apparently tried to cross the good copper sometime in the past. One was found bounded, gagged and crow eaten near Mt Kosciuszko. The other was purportedly anchored at the bottom of Port Phillip Bay feeding the marine life. Not that Nick put great faith in the stories, considering their sources. The smaller the minds, the bigger the stories he'd often found in his eight years as a White Dragon. But whether the stories were wholly true or not, he still feared Copper Harris, especially after his recent driving performance in the Criterion Hotel's car park. It added a new dimension to driving SCUD RAGE at the Intencity Arcade. One dead shooter, to be specific. He was duly warned, though, about fraternising with scab dealers poaching on territory not their own, wasn't he? No, not one to cross on a whim, the good copper. If he went west, Nick vowed, he'd take every precaution necessary to stay out of the detective inspector's headlight range.

The plane touched down on the tarmac as if it had cushions for wheels. As they turned and taxied back towards a terminal that resembled an overgrown shed, Nick picked up on the Copper Harris thread again. His resourcefulness; there was that to consider as well. As the cop shop's master of disguises, he ran with more names than a lost dog. Blind man, formula one driver, hospital patient. A shoo-in for an AFI award if anyone ever decided to turn a film camera his way. After those last performances, anyway, it wouldn't take much on the acting scale for him to play a west coast fisherman, or a meter reader. No, never one to dismiss lightly. The good detective inspector had a habit of turning up anywhere, anytime, as anyone.

The plane gunned its engines suddenly, perhaps as a wake up call to the ground staff, then came to a stop. Shut down, the propellers feathered the air for a moment, then everything went still. As Nick released his seat belt, a hefty, full-bearded native opened the passenger door and rolled down the steps.

'I hope you enjoy your stay on Flinders,' the pilot commented, taking off his headset and looking over his shoulder.

'Thank you, I expect to.' Nick gave the pilot a last smile, then reached for his daypack and made his way to the door.

8

From the blackness a dull feeling emerged. The feeling sharpened, throbbed to a pulse, registered as pain in her head, cheekbone and hand.

There came an image: a syringe squeezed between a man's tattooed fingers. Then, far away at first, came a song –

> And I tell you things aren't quite the same
> Cuz' it makes me feel like I'm a man
> When I put a spike into your vein...

The syringe and fingers swooped closer; the song grew louder. A face hovered over her – Nick's.

His smile beamed down like a magician's. 'From the rubbish bin,' he said, running his tongue over his lips. 'You know which one, don't you?' He cackled in delight and continued his song –

> Cuz' when the smack begins to flow
> Then you really don't care no more...

Nick plunged the needle into her vein.

'NOOooo!'

Jackson's eyes cracked open. Her face was flush against the road. Her head buzzed. Her ears rang. She felt dazed and flashes of pain made her wince. She lay there a minute before rolling slowly over and viewing the whirling trees and hearing the wind again. Her eyes dropped. A bike with panniers was strewn across the dirt road. Just above it, a VW Beetle was stopped, its engine chugging away. The driver's door was open, but no one was in it.

She looked skyward and struggled to find herself here, before rolling on her left side and seeing the snake curled back on itself, a metre away. 'Aaaahh!' she screamed. Pain spread as she dragged herself away.

'Stay there!' a voice shouted from beyond the car. 'The snake's dead! It can't hurt you!'

Heart hammering, she drew herself up into a ball.

Footsteps approached and stopped next to her. A damp cloth stroked her forehead and cheekbone.

The voice was there again. 'Can you lie flat? I've got a blanket rolled up here for you.'

An arm cradled her head and the blanket was slipped in under it. Another arm supported her back as she gradually stretched out and viewed a white-bearded man who she'd seen before, but couldn't recall where.

He was on his knees now, placing the cloth over her forehead. 'How're you feeling?'

'Head's sore. My cheek and hand hurt too.' It was then that she noticed her sleeves and pant legs had been rolled up.

'Right. Well, you're talking, seeing and hearing all right, so I reckon you've just been concussed. Your cheek and hand have got some skin missing. But from the way you moved yourself up the road just now, I don't think any bones are broken.' He paused to glance at the snake, then ran his fingers up and down her arms. 'That tiger snake took a swipe at you. But I can't see any marks or swelling. So either he missed, or your clothes protected you. They're rear-fanged, you know, so that can happen.'

It was his quiet voice and far away look that fired her memory. 'You were the one in the hotel. We talked, didn't we?'

'We did, yes. It augers well you can remember that.'

Looking over at the panniers, she remembered more – what was in one of them.

'We should get you in the car. There's a medical centre in Whitemark. They'll be able to have a closer look at you.'

Jackson raised herself onto her elbows. Everything was in focus one moment, then blurred the next. She felt suddenly nauseous. 'It's just a bump on the head and a few scratches. I'm right. I don't want to go there,' she said sharply, before lowering herself back down.

'Right then. I'll take you back to the hotel. There's a doctor just around the corner, in case you change your mind.'

'No, not there, either.' She struggled to raise herself again, but nausea flattened her. 'If I can just get to the shack… Do you know where Bushed Out is?' Her brain felt drugged and refused to clear.

'I know the gate. It's just up ahead.'

'That's…' She lost the thread of what she wanted to say for a moment. 'That's where I want to go.'

Wind gusted again.

She found the keys and handed them to him. 'For the locks on the gate and door. Can you just get me there?' she asked, her voice growing distant to her. A fog – the colour of the sun – settled over her. His face and the trees started to shimmer, then retreat.

'All right.' Pete stood, went over and lifted up the bike and panniers. 'Handlebars are twisted. The back brakes aren't working.'

It felt as though she were in a huge balloon rising up from the road. Her eyes closed; her mind dimmed and she streaked back into the void – black and silent.

Pete lifted the kickstand with his foot. 'I'll move this off the road, then we'll see about getting you to Bushed Out.'

She didn't hear.

9

Jackson woke again, not knowing where she was. Light came from the lantern hanging from the roof, and there was the smell of kerosene and dust. Night, she realised, before turning her head.

Sitting on a chair close to her was a young, solidly built bloke, with thick ginger hair and a broad, freckled face. He was reading a magazine with a horse and spindly-legged foal on the cover. Though she had no idea who he was, his clothes comforted her. The overalls, flannel shirt and rubber boots meant he had to be from somewhere nearby.

She glanced around trying to get her bearings. A blanket was tucked tight across her chest. With her hands stacked over her stomach, she felt like a corpse at her own funeral. That left hand, she noticed, was bandaged. A wood stove spat behind her. Memory flashes came. Wind. Trees. Bicycle. Unending dirt road. The snake and that old man. Then it hit her where she was. Stupid woman. Even in the darkness, with half a brain left, she should have recognised Bushed Out.

She looked back over at the stranger and thought he wasn't much older than she was. Perhaps he was the old man's son.

Lifting his head, he caught her staring at him and put on a tentative grin. 'Hi.'

'Hi. Who are you?'

It took him a moment to answer, like he had to think about it. 'John. And you?'

'Jackson.' 'It augers well you can remember that,' was what the old man had said on the road. Why was that in her head?

'Interesting name.'

'A product of eccentric parents… The name, I mean. I'm adopted.'

She fell into silence wondering why she'd said that. A rattled brain, she decided finally, feeling her forehead for any noticeable leaks or cracks.

His eyes flicked around the room before landing back on her again. 'How're you feeling?'

'Dazed, a bit sore. Why are you here?'

'Well, I…I live fairly close by. Well, for parts of the year anyway. And I'm just here to watch over things until Pete and my father get back.'

'By things, you mean me?'

He nodded to indicate he did.

She eyed the panniers near his feet. Both were still full. 'Where'd they go?'

'To drop that bike of yours off in town.'

Alarm pricked her. 'At night?'

John nodded again. 'Business hours are pretty flexible on the island.'

'I could've taken it back.'

'Yeah, well… Maybe in a day or two you could have.' He paused to look at his feet and collect more words. 'The doctor's been out to have a look at you and recommended plenty of rest.'

'Okay… So how'd I get in here?'

'You gave Pete your keys. He drove over and got us and we got you into the back of our flat-tray and brought you here. It was only a hundred metres or so.'

A wind gust buffeted the windows. She could feel the draught through the window frame.

'So Pete lives nearby?'

'At the end of the road, in a shack out on the point. He leases it from my father.'

'Ah. I've seen it…once.'

'That'd be enough, I reckon. It's not the sort of place you'd have a second look at unless you had a people allergy, which I s'pose Pete does.' He stood up and moved to the sink. 'Anyway, like a drink?'

'Tea would be good.'

When John returned with the drinks minutes later, she was out to it again, so he sat back down exchanging the mugs for his magazine and continued to read and watch over her.

10

Pete sat on a rock on the seaward side of his shack and watched with a mixture of curiosity and discomfort as Jackson crossed the sand heading his way.

When she got close, she stopped and called out to him, 'Good morning.'

'Morning.' What he said next came straight from Santi. 'The doors are open. You can come through if you like.' Only the grazier and his son ever had.

Jackson entered hesitantly, surveying the place as she went through – the scuffed carpet, hessian curtains, small table, chairs and single bed. A daypack and clothes hung from hooks by the door. A faded tea towel and pots were on the kitchen wall at the other end, where fish sizzled away on his wood stove. In between, a sketchpad, pencils and books filled the only shelf. Above the bed were three framed photographs. She slowed long enough to look at them. The largest one in the middle was a wedding photo showing a grinning, thin-faced man in a suit with his hands clasped in front of him and his hair spilling over his ears. Beside him, arm in his, was an Asian girl in a white pantsuit. Her long, flowing hair was laced with small flowers and she had a bright, upturned smile. To the left of that photo, two young boys were digging away in sand. The photo on the right showed older boys knee-deep in surf, arms around their surfboards. Their eyes bulged and their mouths were agape as though they were posing for a JAWS poster. Him in the middle photo, she decided. His family too, somewhere else now.

She moved out the back door just as he tossed something towards a nearby rock. Small birds with spiked tail feathers swooped on it, feeding and squeaking away.

He turned to her. 'Good to see you on your feet again. You looked untroubled coming over the sand. So you must be feeling all right.'

'Yes… That boy, John, told me you lived out here. So I've just come to thank you for helping me.'

Pete nodded and motioned towards the flat rock beside him. 'The doctor who looked in on you last night did say you'd need to rest. Why don't you sit down.'

She did. The rock was still night cool and free of droppings. She turned and looked out at the broad sweep of ocean just beginning to move their way in the light breeze. The beach to her left was an empty arc of sand that sloped gently up to the coastal scrub and trees. Eyeing it, a thought formed. She'd spotted a shovel leaning against his shack as she came in. If she could get a hold of it, it would take about ten minutes to bury the heroin in the soft soil. That done, she'd be free to return to Whitemark: well, after arranging for some form of transport to get there.

Pete stood up. 'Like some breakfast?'

'I had something earlier.' A mug of tea was the something.

'Plenty of fish in the pan. Like an egg with it?'

Perhaps he hadn't heard her. 'Okay,' she relented, thanking him again.

Pete brought out the fish and an egg, a slice of bread and a mug of tea. She was hungry and ate quickly, looking up occasionally to glimpse the back of his head as he stared out at the ocean.

'Good food,' she said once.

He stayed quiet.

She suspected he felt even more awkward than she did. Finished, she tried again. 'I can't remember if I introduced myself.' When he didn't respond, she gave him her name and added, 'I've come over from Melbourne to do some concentrated exam study.'

He gave a nod and his name, which of course she already knew. Then there was just the ocean for him again.

She wondered if he were expecting a visitor to arrive by boat.

'There was a bloke in town last night asking around for you,' he said finally, not bothering to look around.

'Oh?' she uttered. Anything more and her voice would have betrayed her. She waited, anxious for him to go on.

'Pointy face, red hair, goatee.' The shock sent her breathless.

'"Could talk a feral cat off a fish truck" was how Bowman at the service station described him.'

Her alarm bordered on panic. Then Ben was in terrible trouble. She felt she had to say something, but what? 'Did…did you tell him where I was?'

He turned her way finally. 'I didn't meet him. Apparently he spoke to Bowman earlier. It was Bowman who told us about him.'

She couldn't stop herself. 'Did anybody tell him where I was?' She tried to disguise her feelings, sound light and casual, but doubted she did.

Pete sipped on his tea before answering. 'Bowman thought you'd biked south and mentioned that to him. After renting a car, the bloke headed off that way. So if there wasn't anybody pub-bound for Lady Barron who saw you riding across the island, he'll probably think that's where you are, or have been anyway.' Pete's eyes held hers. 'The island's small, as you know, so it shouldn't take him long to work out you're somewhere else. If you like, I could run you down there.'

No choice, she had to answer. 'No, thanks.'

He nodded, as seemed his habit. 'Right, then.' He stood up and walked past her back into the shack, where he found his daypack and went around putting things into it. 'I'm just going for a walk down the beach.' He paused a moment before asking, 'Like to come along?'

'Only as far as the road. I've plenty of study to do. I'd better get back.'

Relief quickened his response. 'Okay.'

After they parted, Pete tracked along the shoreline thinking how strange it felt dwelling on someone outside his family – well, someone in the flesh anyway. 'Remember that grade ten girl, the one who knocked on our door that time?' he said to Santi. 'Bridget Saunders her name was. A top kid with a tree swinger for a father we later learned. Remember her under the porch light that night, her swollen face stilled in shock? Unable to say anything, do anything but stare at us until you brought her in and sat her down. Did you notice this girl's face when I mentioned that bloke who'd been asking around for her? The same look as Bridget Saunders'. And how she reacted on the road yesterday when I offered to take her back into Whitemark. You don't have to be an ASIO operative to work it out, do you? She's on the run. From that…how did Bowman put it? 'Big city lad with the gift of the gab.'

He skirted up past the first low-tide lagoon and went into the trees. There he sat against a tree trunk and stared at the sunlight shifting along the ground in front of him. He spotted a blue-tongue lizard looking perplexed about why its spot of sun wouldn't stay still. Pete explained the problem to it, then wished he'd brought his sketchbook along when sunlight struck the lizard again. In his early days out here, such bush-cloistered occurrences held little interest for him. But now they did. He was managing his life better, walking less and sitting around staring at the detail of things more: textures, colours, this sort of shifting light and shadow. He'd bought writing pads and biros, drawing pencils and a sketchbook in town. Nowadays he wrote a little and sketched a lot. Perhaps it all had to do with learning to live with himself, albeit slowly. Well, during the daylight hours anyway. Nights were still long. The inlet's intense loneliness still hit him hard then, though not quite as hard as before.

Minutes later, he decided to return to the shack to get his sketchbook and pencils. He rose stiffly and moved out on to the open sand. Looking up, he stopped suddenly. Someone was at the back of the shack. He got his binoculars out, used them and recognised the girl as she started walking over rock and sand towards the nearest line of trees. She held a daypack in one hand, his shovel in the other. When he lost sight of her, he stashed his binoculars, stepped back into the scrub and headed her way.

11

True, she hadn't had a lot of contact with her adopted niece over the years, especially after Geoff and Margaret broke up. But Louise knew that this big city blow-in – cleavage-fixated and fawning all over her twenty-four hours earlier – would hold about as much attraction for Jackson as a tiger snake in mating season. So why was he back here being so persistent in looking for her? Especially since she was on the island to isolate herself and study. You didn't need advanced psychology skills to dismiss his spiel about being Jackson's boyfriend's best mate here to research an article for *Australia – Living It Together* magazine.

'Have you tried down at Lady Barron?' Louise asked in her most earnest voice, wiping down the bar for the third time and vowing to head out to Bushed Out the instant her shift finished. She knew this glue-grinning reject had been down to Lady Barron; she'd got word. Fortunately, with the exception of Bowman and that Patriarch sandman, it seemed no one else had taken any notice of Jackson, either here or while she was riding over to the east coast.

'As a matter of fact, I have,' Nick answered congenially. 'After leaving this magnificent hotel yesterday, I stayed there last night and asked around for her but, sadly, no luck. It was worth the trip down though for the stunning coastal scenery and stimulating conversation alone. Both of which I plan to feature in my article.' That manic smile assailed her. He placed his hands on the bar and leaned forward, halving the distance between them. 'The thing is, Miss…?

She knew how to play his game. 'Minogue.' She slipped the wedding ring off her finger. Catching his dropped eyes ogling her again, she stepped back.

'Of course. I can pick the resemblance. Sisters, surely. And you'd have
be the younger one.'

'Cousins, actually.' The threatened onset of nausea prevented her from
going on.

'Ah. Well, the thing is, Miss Minogue, I have strong reason to believe
Jackson was coming here first before going anywhere else on island.'

'Sorry,' she said quickly, shaking her head and shrugging her shoulders.
'I didn't see anyone like her here last night or this morning either.' And
she hadn't. 'You'll have to excuse me a moment.' She began to move down
the bar, sponge in hand. 'The cleaning's like the wind in here. It just never
seems to stop.'

Wind? Nick thought to himself. Inside the hotel? The place felt
draught-free to him. Watching her burn a path to the opposite end of the
bar, Nick took out a ciggy and lit up. Gave the same answers as all the
other boofhead islanders, didn't she? But was unique in her discomfort
level and hunger for space after she did. So, two conclusions: a less than
honest character and she had crossed the girlfriend's path recently.

Why the boys in blue persisted in using lie detectors to grill society's
scumbag brigade remained a mystery to him. It was a sad waste of taxpayers'
money, their reliance on gadgetry rather than the simple power of the
eye. Body language. That was the key. Observe it closely, as you would
a glossy-paged skin mag, X-rated video or Internet site, while always
remaining mindful of future applications. A stark shortage of such viewing
opportunities around this place, though, he thought, sampling his beer and
gazing out the window at the many Bowman businesses across the road.

As the front bar's only customer, he thought she'd have stayed close,
offered to light up his ciggy and provided some social discourse. While
admittedly not treasure troves of information about Jackson, or anything
else remotely a part of the real world, at least the broad-arsed clones he'd
met down at Lady Barron were prepared to feign an interest in him,
asking where he was from and whether he was enjoying his stay. In Nick's
book, that counted for a lot in places far away from home. But this lady
— it was like he stood there before her a free-bleeder with HIV from the

way she reacted after he'd put on his best smile and popped the questions. All head action she was – shaking it, dropping it and turning it to spot the nearest conversation escape. Such actions brought to mind his mentor back when Nick was on his L plates in the business. 'Eye contact,' Copper Harris had preached. 'The true barometer of effective communication. Absolutely essential in the service industry.' And ever since then, Nick had adhered to that good advice. But this one had a serious attitude problem, didn't she? Obviously needed a refresher course in hospitality to remedy it. A pity he didn't have the time to give it to her. He ran his tongue over his lips and belched loudly.

Anyway, where was he? Eye contact, yeah, that was it. It was hard not to warm to this, a favourite topic that served as a continual theme for his motivation talks to that icon of multicultural business enterprise – the White Dragons – as well as to their back-seat bank artists. 'You speak equally with your eyes,' he told them. 'So no matter your level of discomfort in dealing with people, the thing you must realise is that proper intercourse – social or otherwise – always requires a meeting of the eyes.' He thought there was a touch of the poet in that last bit: well, when he got the rhythm right, anyway.

He popped his knuckles and crooned, 'Where are you, Jackson?' just to test his hearing.

Her with the watermelon hooters had obviously seen her, so the girlfriend was here, but not any more. Lady Barron didn't have her. She wasn't on the previous day's return flights he'd paid that Flintstone terminal attendant to enquire about. So, unless she owned A-grade swimming skills, she still had to be holed up somewhere on this museum piece of an island. As he sucked on his ciggy and swigged his beer, his eyes ran over the wood panel wall in front of him. They settled on a crayfish-shaped map. It would follow, then, that she'd stay away from the main road and the fish-reeking settlements further north. Stroking his goatee, he squinted and eyed a fine-line road that wove east almost as far as the coast. He took note of where it ended – nowhere. 'Gotcha,' he said, grinning.

12

That road, his defence line against the outer world, was being breached. In strife, this girl had buried the source of her troubles in the trees not more than a hundred metres from where Pete sat now. And in another few days, she'd be gone, leaving behind her real purpose for coming here. And whatever it was she'd buried was sure to attract others in, like crows to carrion, sometime. He sipped his tea, watching the ocean and speculating on what was under that loose earth and marker rock, and who it would draw in first. The man with the red goatee, and others like him? So, should he grab the shovel and unearth what was buried? Or would it be better to walk over to Bushed Out and, using his gravest principal's voice, admit he'd seen her and allow ensuing silence to claw away at her conscience in the hope she'd decide to tell him the whole story.

The sound of an approaching vehicle – a Beetle, so probably one of Bowman's – put a decision on hold and got him thinking about ending his lease and looking for a place up around Northeast River.

Minutes later, the green Beetle stopped at the end of the road. Pete watched the man get out and marvelled at how quickly one of his questions had been answered.

*

Not the sort of bloke I've had call to do a great deal of business with, Nick thought, leaving the east coast. Next to him, that scaly, jelly-eyed set down at Lady Barron were poet laureates. Still, the old mollusc did retain a mastery of the island's favourite word – No – didn't he? Well, in word if not in eye contact. Anyway, enough of this joy. Time for a strategy change. In name – Plan B, The Escape of the Smack Poacher. Ooooee! Film title extraordinaire! Write that one down, number one!

Now where was I? Oh yeah, ringing up base camp with a heavily edited update. After that, day trip back to Saintland. Hair dye what's above the tooth hole, shave what's below it. Stolen credit card purchase a new camera, binoculars, sunnies, shorts and West Coast Eagles cap, before arranging for the break-out of boyfriend Ben, as well as a personal tagger – at an hourly rate – to track his movements. An hour should do it. With his veins boiling for a regulation fix, there's little doubt where he'll bolt to next. And as I've always judged myself a better watcher than tracker, director than actor, I'll sit outside the local café here that specialises in road kill stew – though the fish and chips will do me – and await his arrival. Later, I might even skip up to the hotel for dessert. Then, after a good night's sleep, it'll just be a matter of where the boyfriend leads me.

*

Pete sat down on his rock with a fresh mug of tea. Watching the waves, he muttered, 'What to do?'

Santi's voice was soon in his head. 'You used to call it taking the bit between the teeth when you got involved with staff and student problems back up in Blackall.'

'I did, yes.'

'And as you've said before, this girl's obviously on the run, and what's buried over there has got to be the cause.'

'Uh huh.'

'And it's already started drawing people in.'

'It has, yes.'

'It seems to me you've got two options, Pete.'

'Which are?'

'Stay crippled by the past and find yourself another beach cave, or take the bit between your teeth and find out what she's buried.' Santi wasn't always soft and soothing.

'No hiding which option you're going for.'

After a minute, he got up, collected his shovel and walked into the nearby trees.

*

ANGLICAN ARCHBISHOP SUPPORTS SAFE INJECTING ROOMS

'Jesus H. Johnson,' Detective Inspector Harris mumbled to himself, glancing out at a banner sheet newspaper headline while coming over the Westgate Bridge. 'Next they'll be advocating stocking smack on supermarket shelves. Or issuing licences and marketing it through the Internet. Welcome to EASYSCORE. Simply enter your credit card details on the line below. Bloody typical of this government. Making everything permissible so their fingers can stretch deeper into taxpayers' pockets to fill up their own.'

No point in dwelling on all this now, though, with holidays just hours away, he thought. After a couple of city phone calls, it would be time to shut the vault on everything down here – minutes of Crimestoppers' meetings, police reports, profit margins – and board the Flying Kangaroo for the Gold Coast. He let his mind drift northwards and pictured himself in shorts, sunnies and an I LOVE SURFERS T-shirt wandering around taking in what was on offer, before purchasing some of it.

Whatever was accessible and comfortable for the passing tourist trade was good enough for him. Though, like everyone else, he did have his fetishes. Skimpily clad blondes – barely out of school uniform, sun-baked and jobless – were his first choice. Their illusions shattered, it came down to daily survival money for them, or a hit-up or two. He was happy to provide either for the right response. And in such a competitive market as Surfers', they'd had to learn fast and well what that was.

When he tired of the young and desperate, he'd set his sights on a few beyond their apprenticeship years, and all that that entailed. He'd heard reports from recent returnees about how good places like Bangkok, Manila, and lately Phnom Penh and Ho Chi Minh City were. But such reports irked him. Keeping Australian business in Australia and supporting local industries had always been two of his highest priorities. True blue he was, and true blue he expected others to be.

Minutes later, Harris drove up Elizabeth Street and spotted a safe phone box. He stopped in a loading zone, switched on his flashing lights and got out. First priority was mystery man Nick. He'd chased that loose supply to some rock in Bass Strait. And though he'd logged in three short sentences on the answering machine ('Still island-bound. Language and landscape are requiring extra study. Give me a few more days'), he was overdue with the details. As far as Harris could remember, that had never happened before. Talk was what Nick did, forty-eight hours a day.

Harris stepped in the phone box and dialled Nick's number for the fifth time in the last two days.

'Hello, sport fans. Nick here. I'm indisposed at the moment, either at the pub, having a…'

Harris hung up. Thoughts of his holiday faded as he glared at the phone, listening to the street noise. Feeling an instinct-rush coming on, he stuffed cotton balls up his nostrils, emitted a few practice greetings in his best Toorak voice, then took a phone number book out of his coat pocket and looked up Footscray. Having long delegated storeman's duties to someone else, it had been years since he'd put in his own order, and he wondered if the old number was still applicable.

After the third ring, a gruff voice answered, 'Yeah.'

'Dream time?'

A few seconds passed before the reply came. 'Dream time's now.'

'Eastern Force.' It was like something out of a World War Two spy film.

'Computer's on. Details are showing. Book's open. Go.'

'Four crates of New Guinea Gold and a question.'

'I can verify the Gold. What's the question?'

'I've been out of town and I need to contact my business partner – one Nick Jones. You haven't crossed paths with him in the last week or so, have you?'

'Mmm. Tough one that. With sales running at a brisk pace, lots of names have brushed over the desk lately. Such has been the demand that, once your order is covered, only eight crates of Gold remain from last year's inventory. And for this afternoon only, I can offer them, along with a complimentary methamphetamine pack, at twenty-five per cent off. Interested?'

Harris expected this *if* information was forthcoming. 'Yes. I'd be grateful if you could add them to my order.'

'With pleasure. Now, to one Nick Jones. I do seem to recall something. Ah, yes. You're aware of his recovery work on Flinders Island?'

'I am.'

'Then you obviously know about the powder poacher who's been putting in some small-room time here.'

'Yes, I know about him.'

'Right. Street rumour has it he got his discharge papers this morning and is off to that very same island your mate Nick Jones is touring. The only other item being muted about is a sale coming our way once Nick returns. But, as you two share the same business card, I expect you already know about that one.'

Harris's jaw felt like an iron clamp. A terrible urge came over him to smash his fist into something. 'Yes. Yes, I do,' he forced himself to say.

'That's all I've got, then. Sorry.'

'It's enough. I'm just pleased to know everything's going according to the script. I'll expect him back in a couple of days then. Thanks for your help.' He hung up and put a hand inside his coat, stroking the butt end of his revolver and breathing deeply for a full minute.

If his business could be compared with a chess game, then Nick had suddenly jumped from a pawn to a knight – unseen, unsolicited, unapproved. In chess, as in business, the penalty for such a rule contravention is the same – immediate displacement. Harris rang up Qantas and cancelled his booking.

13

Ben was agitated. His body itched and tingled with fever. Tiny beads of sweat broke out on his forehead. Nausea would follow soon if he didn't do something about it.

After checking there weren't any mainland faces he knew here, he grabbed his daypack off the trolley, went inside the airport and located the men's toilet. Given the way he was feeling, he'd chase the dragon first, *then* wash up and change his shirt. No needle, but he had some foil, a cigarette lighter and a straw. So in he went. Fortunately, no one was about. He locked the door, went into a cubicle and stretched the foil out over the toilet bowl. He heated up his last bit of smack until it started to smoke and curl. Using the straw, he snorted it quickly, and within seconds he lifted and started to feel good for the first time in days.

He strolled back out into the foyer with a vision in his mind of Jack waiting for him at the hotel. She was sitting in an ancient lounge chair, head tipped into the palm of her hand. A musty carpet covered the floor. A chandelier hung from the roof.

'Jack.'

Her rich brown eyes – like swollen chocolate drops – rose to view him. They stayed dull, devoid of expression, though, and rightly so. Disapproval showed on her face.

He dropped to his knees in front of her and took out the silver bracelet he'd had in his pocket for days. 'You saved me, Jack.' He took her hand and fastened the bracelet around her wrist. 'In a day or two, I'll contact my one-off suppliers and explain that hiccups happen.' (No sense recounting how much of a hiccup his Dragon stay had been.) 'Knowing that the merchandise is safe (well, less a tweezer pinch for coming off of it purposes), they'll forgive and forget. I know they will.'

Outside the terminal, everything glittered in gold sequins. The sea breeze was fresh, the sun warm on his face. Between the noisy sea and distant mounds of hills, there were low trees and empty space.

'What a call, Jack!' he whooped to the wind-slanted scrub. That image of them at the hotel returned. His voice lowered. 'Where we've been the last few days, Jack, makes where we're going twice as important, so our new page together starts now.'

He vowed to himself to call things off with Bee, and with Lan too, when he got back home. No way would they have done what Jack had for him. Who would have? So what a good girl she was. So good, in fact, their future together *had* to occupy more than just a new page. The entire book had to be new and entitled *Strictly Monogamy*. He smiled, muttering, 'I never thought I'd ever agree to that. Jack.'

He heard a car approach and slow down behind him. A wave of unease gripped him, before a voice rang out, 'Need a lift into town?'

*

Sipping a cappuccino outside the Whitemark café, Nick put his three-day-old newspaper down and started giving some thought to his golfing future. The dozen Greg Norman-autographed balls he'd lost during his morning round of golf at the local course was a source of considerable embarrassment to him. Especially as it was witnessed by that pond life behind him continually yelping something about wanting to 'go through', then going apeshit when he sent back his two-finger reply. Anyway, it was the most energy he'd seen expended out of anyone here since that no-tongue bar lady walked all the way up the bar and back again serving him his beer last time he was in.

Besides the lost balls and having his performance witness stamped by those wankers, there was the small matter of whether to buy his own clubs and join a golf club over there on far western shores. With the escalating costs of equipment and appropriate apparel, he reckoned he might have to re-negotiate the smack contract during his final stopover in Saintland. Though things hadn't been all that tidy there twenty-four hours earlier when he mentioned he'd forgotten to calculate the GST in the original costing. If he hadn't complete faith in their ability to appreciate the smack sale of the century price – GST or no GST – he might have taken more notice of their scowling faces and low, private murmurings. As it was, he still had little doubt they'd be kissing his toes and naming a warehouse after him.

Having heard the plane go over ten minutes earlier, Nick's thoughts shifted to the man of the moment. At first he thought the antique car that pulled up at the hotel housed the boyfriend. It took so long for the passenger to get out, Nick thought the driver might have to put in a call for community service assistance. And word had it, over the waters, that the smack-head poacher had noticeably slowed in his post-confinement movements. So when an old bloke eventually did cast his shadow on late afternoon sunlight, Nick felt a twinge of concern. He ran his thumb and forefinger down his goatee, realised it wasn't there, then told himself the boyfriend had to have been on that plane, and he had to come to this hotel before going anywhere else.

Convinced by the logic of his argument, Nick finished his cappuccino, clicked his fingers and shouted, 'Oy!' When no one came, he shouted again. Finally he got up and, stumbling over an old FOR SALE OR LEASE sign, went in and gave the place a full-volume wake-up call. When the proprietor eventually lumbered out, it passed Nick's mind that an opium den could've been operating in the back, as dopey as mein host looked. This time Nick ordered two cappuccinos to spare him the pain of having to do it all over again. 'Jesus H. Johnson! This place couldn't win a service award in a one-entry competition!' were his last words, as he handed over his hard-earned money and latched on to his drinks. Mein host gave him a Neanderthal grunt and headed back to bed.

Eleven minutes later, a small humped car rattled up to the front of the hotel.

This time the smack-head poacher-in less than mint condition – did alight on recognisably lightened feet. Geez, he'd thinned down since coming off the hospital food, Nick observed on second glance. Anyway, to the trained eye there was little doubt what he was using for sustenance now. A few hours float time, the lure of a long sleep on a regulation bed, some compulsory itch and scratch over his morning corn flakes, and the jumpy boyfriend would be perched on Bowman's doorstep right on the chime of opening time.

Nick looked over at his own Bowman Beetle parked against the curb, then he picked up his new Nikon Coolpix 995 digital camera and activated the times four 38–152 zoom lens. He put it to his eye and looked skyward. It could pick out rock formations on the moon as easily as it had boyfriend Ben cosying up to a Saintland smack supply; the details of which would be duly pointed out to him and Action Jackson at wherever Ben led him to the next day. The photos would ensure that the smack-poacher's loss was his long-term gain. There might even be an opportunity to snap a commemorative photo or two just to complete the collection, Nick considered as an afterthought.

He scanned the town's low, colourless buildings and watched them tinge a pale yellow, the glare of the sun bright against their windows. Two schoolchildren rode their bikes, tinkling handlebar bells, down the middle of the road. No other sounds were out there, just the bells.

'Ah, this Whitemark street life,' Nick swooned to himself. 'Like an oil painting in the softening light, is it not, number one?' And at that moment in time, he felt there was nowhere else in the world he'd rather be. He picked up his newspaper, scanned the stock market report without understanding any of it, then finished his cappuccinos and leaned back. 'What better way to top off this feeling of utter contentment,' he muttered, 'than to step over to that fine pub for a couple of pre-retirement beers.' It wasn't a journey he thought he'd take again after his previous experience there. But such was his magnanimous view of the world now that he was prepared to forgive and forget past slights: well, those suffered away from the local golf course anyway. So over to the pub he went.

*

The books barely merited a look. Each time Jackson sat down with them, she lasted only a minute or two before springing up to sweep the floor, or dust the window ledges, or bring more wood inside. But all this busyness seemed useless, for it couldn't get her mind off Ben, and that evil bastard Nick. When she heard the knock on the door, she froze initially, before creeping over to the front window and peeking out. Seeing big, lumbering John outside sent a surge of relief through her. She opened the door and invited him in, thanking him for what he'd done for her.

He sat down where he had before and declined her offer of a drink. 'I've got a baby wombat in the back of the flat-tray that I'm taking home, so I can't stay long.'

She sat down opposite him. 'Really?' She couldn't help smiling. 'What do you plan to do with it?'

'Take care of it. Its mother was killed on the road.' He told her that he looked after injured animals; vet science in Launceston and during the holidays he worked part-time for the local vet at Lady Barron. Like her, he had to return in a few days to sit exams also.

She welcomed the distraction. 'How many injured animals have you got at the moment?'

'With the one on the flat-tray, three. There's another small wombat and a young wallaby that are about ready for release. When the wombats are a year old, they can fend for themselves. So Dad and I take them out and reintroduce them into the bush.'

Incredible, Jackson thought. Packing in smack, then talking wombats. 'Don't you miss them when they're gone?'

His eyes found the floor. 'I must admit, I do get a bit upset sometimes.' He looked up moments later. 'Anyway, what I came here to say was that Dad and I were at the hotel earlier. Louise, um, your aunt is on her own behind the bar and things are busy there.' He stopped, for no other reason it seemed than to smile awkwardly at her.

'Right.' She waited.

'Anyway, Louise asked if one of us could drop by and tell you that a bloke named Ben something checked in at the hotel this afternoon. She gave him your message.'

'Oh right,' Jackson said with forced casualness. 'Thanks for that.' Then why wasn't Ben out here now?

'And she said one other thing as well. The bloke with the red goatee, the one she told you about when she was out here earlier in the week…' He paused for an acknowledgement.

'Right.' She shifted uneasily.

'Well, a bloke was in at the pub last night. Clean-shaven, dark hair, but with a voice and mannerisms the same as his. Louise thought it was sort of strange, that maybe they were the same person, and she thought you ought to know.'

Jackson felt her blood chill. 'Thanks.'

He mulled something else over for a moment. 'Listen, I…I sometimes take a wombat or two for a walk along the beaches around here. Actually, I should do that again today. So I could come back out here in…in an hour or so and maybe you'd like to walk along with us… I mean, if you feel up to it, that is.' He gazed at her, hopeful.

'Fine, okay.' Her mind was lodged somewhere else.

*

Regretting having agreed to this walk, Jackson was intent on making it quick, but it was she who soon fell behind. Legs like pylons below a thick body and arms, John ploughed his way through the sand taking one step for every two of hers. Reining himself in when she fell behind, he apologised and asked how she was feeling before picking up the pace again. Soon, in his self perceived role as tour guide, he delivered a non-stop monologue on the local plant and bird life, especially the mutton-birds on some nearby island. Topics so far removed from her own world and immediate preoccupations that she couldn't help smiling at the huge disparity between what she was thinking and what they were doing. Though at times she only half-listened – concerned as she was about Ben and Nick – she began to welcome his idle chatter. When he stopped finally, she took off her shoes, rolled up her jeans and went wading in the water.

John took off his boots and waded in as well, staying close. 'I love this,' he said, watching the wavelets sweep in. 'Everything's moving and nobody else is here.'

That caught her. She gazed up at him. That gawky manner of his obviously had little to do with the way he viewed things. Squinting against the brightness, she looked down the beach that stretched far out in front of them. Wheeling gulls, wind-driven sea and spray; and little spirals of sand moving over the dunes. He was right, and she told him so, and compared this to Melbourne where everything moved because half the country's population lived there, or so it seemed to her. Feeling less a stranger to him now, Jackson shelved her worries, for the moment anyway.

As they began to walk back, heads lowered against the wind, she noticed the wombat nosing the sand as though scouring for food. 'What do you feed your wombats?' she asked, initiating conversation for the first time.

'Whatever we've got growing around the place. This time of the year, we…' And on he went, this budding Patriarch Tour Guide, this island-bound Doctor Harry, walking and talking about his wombat-by-the-seasons' feeding program, pausing only long enough to ask how she was feeling, as if she were some beach-walking invalid.

Nearing the end of the road, John went quiet suddenly. Talked out or tongue-tied? Jackson couldn't tell. She stopped and eyed Pete's place further on, then looked up at John again. Tongue-tied, she decided, when she caught him smiling a message at her that read, I'd like to ask you something, but I could suffer a panic attack doing it. He glanced away; his face taking on a concerned look.

Her thoughts switched back to Ben and Nick. 'I think I might detour to Pete's. I want to ask him something.' She wasn't about to mention what that something was, thereby encouraging him, so she thanked him and started to walk away.

'Can I come by again,' he blurted out. 'Uh, just to check that you're all right and…everything. Tomorrow, or maybe the next day?'

All she could think to say was 'If you want.' Then she added, 'I might not be here, though.'

'Right. Well, if you are, maybe we could do something.'

She backed away. 'Maybe.'

'Okay, bye.'

'Bye.' She felt suddenly deflated. Things were getting very complicated again. She turned and continued to Pete's place.

*

Pete inserted his short knife, searched out the hinge and prised open the oyster to reveal its tender flesh. He placed it with others in a plastic bowl at his feet and looked out at a sea eagle moving off the water, its afternoon catch firmly fastened in its long talons. He watched it lift, then soar on the thermals like a great white butterfly before dropping its payload and spiralling down in free-fall to grab the fish again an instant before it hit the water. As the eagle rose a second time, Pete watched its shadow pass over the ocean.

He picked up his mug of tea finally, took a sip and glanced at the brick-shaped bag of white powder next to him. 'What to do now, eh? Try another walk, heading north this time?'

'The answer wasn't out there before,' Santi reminded him.

'No.' Coincidentally, he spotted Jackson, alone, walking towards the shack, while John moved up towards the road. It seemed the decision had been made for him. He went inside and stowed the daypack and bag under the bed, then returned to his rock.

Jackson avoided the doors this time and rock-hopped up to him. 'I don't mean to disturb you, but I was just wondering when you might be going into Whitemark again?'

'I don't know. Why don't you come in and have a drink and we'll talk about it.' He noticed the anxious look on her face. 'Come on. I'll heat up the kettle.'

She trailed him to the door, then stopped. 'Actually, I think I'll pass on the drink.'

He watched a play of dust in the sunlight streaming through the window. 'You might want to reconsider after I show you something.' He knelt down and pulled out her daypack.

Shocked, her stare turned child-like.

'What we need to do is talk. It's your decision where.'

He followed her outside and sat down, an arm's length away.

'So what's in the bag?'

What could she say? Talcum powder? Or powdered milk buried there in case the world's milk industry suddenly shut down? It had to be obvious what it was. 'Heroin.' She hated the word. She looked out to sea and waited for him to erupt.

He didn't. 'Yours?'

'My boyfriend's.'

'Tell me why you brought it here.' There was nothing reproachful in his voice.

Her eyes stayed on the ocean as she told him everything.

'That bloke who threatened you at Spencer Street station, and tracked you here, he doesn't sound like the type who'd just pack it in and go back where he came from.'

'I'm sorry. I never intended…'

'I know that.' He stood up. 'Want that drink now?'

'Yes, thanks.'

'One thing about all this, though – when you're mapping out your next move, there's one option I'd prefer you didn't consider.'

'What's that?'

'Leaving the island with the contents of that daypack.'

He came out with the drinks and sat back down. 'I've got an idea. It might sound strange, like something out of a B-grade film script, but if the opportunity presents itself, it could work and it won't harm anyone if we try it.'

She straightened up, feeling suddenly bolstered. In her besieged mind, his use of 'we' was like finding a concrete shelter in a force ten storm.

14

'From drug-dazed to drug-hungry,' Nick muttered to him self, grinning that grin. He thought again how easy it was to track smack-heads with the image of their next hit-up foremost in their minds. And boyfriend Ben was no exception, especially on road once travelled over before. No worries if he temporarily shot out of tracking range up ahead. His banner of Bowman Beetle road dust, and knowing where their end point had to be now, gave Nick the freedom to scan the surroundings and register some daydream time on the possibility of heading east before settling down over there on far western shores. So what about this? Non-stop business class flight to LA. Seek out those Californication girls in the briefest gear. Give them his best smile. Slap his moleskins, tip the Akubra and say, 'G'day.' When their knees buckle, lend them an arm and walk them palm to tight bum towards his Hertz convertible's smooth leather seats. 'Oooeee! I'll carrier-pigeon you a photo, Bowman, ya tooth-faced tin merchant!' Nick shouted out, slapping the steering wheel with both hands.

Minutes later, as the road narrowed, he reclaimed those travel plans and pictured himself cruising Sunset Strip alongside other cool dudes in their slick wheels, checking into funky clubs, rapping and bonding with the heaven-sent crumpet and their soul brothers there. 'Yo braw!' he whooped. His high-five spanked the windscreen just as a hump of squashed fur appeared up ahead. He shot around it, then saw a possum dragging itself down the middle of the road. Stretching out over the steering wheel, he lined his left wheel up with it and hit the possum with a thump. 'Price you pay for visiting your flatmates,' he hooted, as more road kill tested his motoring skills. 'SCUD RAGE, you've got nothin' on this!' he shouted, as if Intencity arcade patrons were there witnessing it all.

Hitting the first pothole nearly skulled him and sent his Beetle shuddering. Celebrity tour shelved for the moment, Nick quickly geared down, weaved sharply around more potholes then continued bumping along as clouds built up and spats of rain fell.

Easing his car around a bend, Nick spotted Ben's Vee-dub a hundred metres further on, parked next to a turn-off. He stopped and reversed back until he found some cover.

A minute later Ben appeared, got back in his car and drove on. No one there to ring the welcome bells for him, obviously. Once Ben disappeared around the next bend, Nick followed. He came to the end of the road where Ben's and the old fossil's Vee-dubs were parked together, looking cosy.

Through an opening in the trees, Nick spotted his quarry. 'It's target man striding over sand towards the shack on the headland. Oooeee. The stuff of awards literary. *The Collected Works of Nick Q. Jones* signed, sealed and soon to be delivered to Sandgroper Press, W of A.' He reached over for his Greg Norman rain gear, Coolpix camera, noose and knife. He tested the knife's switch and marvelled at the serrated blade's length and sharpness. It could slaughter pigs as readily as rip open tyres. Sadly, his time was necessarily limited out here: the pigs would have to wait for another day.

*

They stashed the containers when they heard the car and Jackson watched Ben come across the sand. At the open door, she barely recognised him. He was thin and ashen-faced. His eyes were puffy and red. His mouth was twisted downwards and a worm-like scar ran from his lower lip to his chin.

Jackson reached for him and hugged him hard. 'Ben.' A rush of tears stopped her from saying anything more.

'I got your note at Bushed Out,' he said, trying to control his fidgeting.

'Uh huh.' She let go, eyeing him again for a moment before moving towards Pete sitting at the table. 'There's someone here I want you to meet.'

'And how are we all this morning? Coffee on?'

Fear hit Jackson like an electric shock. Her eyes shot back to see a noose drop around Ben's neck and jerk him backwards. A knife went to his throat.

'Only me,' Nick greeted them, his new face poking around Ben's head. 'On the same mission as your feral-faced boyfriend here.' As he prodded Ben forward, Jackson retreated to the table.

'Now, sweet Jackson, if you would be kind enough to sit next to the old man of the sea there, we'll get the business end of this get together over quickly. And Ben, move in any way not instructed, and I'll lengthen your love bite from lip to earlobe.'

Nick reached into his coat pocket, took out a stack of photos and tossed them on the table. 'Purchased a new camera recently, I'm happy to report. So I'll take this opportunity to share my first efforts with you. As the boyfriend here might vaguely recall, the photos were taken in St Kilda, not far from the soul-soothing sounds of traffic rumbling and people chatting at outdoor cafés. Mastering the lack of natural light was my biggest challenge. But I think you'll agree, the camera shows a remarkable ability to capture the most intimate details, even in the dreariest of confined spaces.'

Ben's eyes and mouth were closed now, his brow damp, his hands trembling.

'The good news is, the photos are yours to keep and view at your leisure. When you do, you'll marvel at the needle-tracked arm and the syringe's light bulb reflections as the droplet of smack is eased into the boyfriend's vein. You'll find fascinating too that tortured look on his face when he realises, yet again, that what's in his vein is nowhere near enough to ease his pain. Has a certain poetic edge to it, don't you think? Anyway, photo lovers, it pleases me to report that copies of this masterly work, with names and details on the back, are sitting in an envelope. Later on today, if I don't make contact with camp headquarters, St Kilda CIB will be receiving their copies compliments of the White Dragons. So, are there any questions?... No. Good. We come now to the main item on the agenda.' His voice lost its banter. 'And Jackson, know that if I'm stuffed about on this one, à la mainland style, you'll force me to do something nasty. Now, retrieve what you so dishonestly brought out here and put it on the table. In name, the smack supply.'

Jackson sat stiffly on the edge of her chair glaring at the knife pressing on Ben's throat. She saw herself then, pinned against the locker, the horror of that needle pricking her skin.

'Eh!' Nick shouted. 'You still with us?'

She nodded, seizing hold of her panic.

'The good gear, the reason we're here, remember? Time now to unveil it, or I'll start reworking the boyfriend's neckline.'

Her humiliation and anger welled up again. Mind made up, she stooped, dragged out a container and put it on the table.

'Of course, under the bed. Where else would you find a quarter of a million dollars worth of the good gear out here, eh? Now, be good enough to open the container and place the contents on the table.'

She did as he instructed, watching his face closely. Any sign of doubt and she'd be back down on that floor fast.

'Looks satisfactory.' He glared over the table at her. 'Haven't had a little dabble in it, have we?… No, of course not. One junk star's enough for anyone to support.' He jerked the noose and bellowed in Ben's ear, 'On your knees, maggot brain!'

A moment later Nick grinned that grin and his voice turned amiable again. 'Sorry. I know this might sound inconsiderate of me, but I just can't pass up another photo opportunity. Similar wattage in here as the last place we did this in, wouldn't you agree, feral-face?'

Releasing the noose, but keeping the knife at Ben's throat, Nick took a small camera out of his coat pocket and snapped a quick photo of the container with Jackson and Pete behind it. 'Faaantastic! A little something more to add to the album and second envelope for the boys in blue, if it's needed,' he crowed, putting his camera away and yanking Ben back up. 'Perhaps, old man, you'll learn to vet your company a bit better out here after this experience.'

He eyed Jackson. 'Now, my lady luscious, put the gear back in the container, screw the top on tight and pass it carefully over to bedtime Ben here… That's it. Steady on, feral-face. That's for Uncle Nick, not you. Geez, we'd better get you outside before your heart gives out.' Nick pulled the trembling Ben back a couple steps.' Aahh, Jackson, now that's not the look of a happy camper.'

He stopped at the door and heaved a dramatic sigh. 'Dear oh dear oh dear. All right, just to set your mind at ease, here's what Uncle Nick's prepared to do.' He took two hundred-dollar notes out of his pocket and tossed them on the floor. 'Meal money for the boyfriend. Steady, feral-face, steady. Not long to go now… I recommend glucodin and valium. In a week or two, Ben'll be back on his surfboard, a bit lighter, but considerably wiser. And one more thing to brighten your heart strings. After a hassle-free flight back to Moorabin, I'm going to make that phone call to camp headquarters. Yes, I agree – two very generous acts. If you must know, a strong compassion gene runs through my family. Take note, though. The envelopes and photos will stay on stand by until the next ice age should any unwanted queries come my way from the boys in blue. A hammer blow to your investment hopes, what's happened here. I know that. But then you're both young, capable, just starting out in life. You'll be right.'

Nick let the noose dangle, but kept the knife at Ben's throat as they backed out the door. 'Have a nice day.'

*

There were no distractions at Bushed Out, nowhere to go, nothing to inject. All Ben could do was lie on Jackson's bed buried under blankets, aching and jerking his body about, while his nose and eyes ran and he shivered, sweated and sneezed. The wind came up. Doors and windows rattled. Creosote fell. When stomach cramps cut in, Ben staggered up to the sink and vomited. He struggled to clean up his mess, before getting back into bed, drawing his knees up and moaning at intervals.

Later, he stormed out the door to the toilet. He returned stooped over and trembling and sprawled back on the bed, waving Jackson away.

She stayed close, though, and covered him up in blankets again. 'How long does this go on for?' she asked, broaching his drug sickness for the first time. She asked three more times before giving up. After putting a plastic bowl next to him, she went outside, sat down on the porch bench and waited for Pete to return from Whitemark.

15

Bloody seats are made for midgets, Nick complained to himself, pissed-off and anxious to get out of the plane. But as he waited for the other passengers to hit the tarmac first, he took comfort in knowing that it would be business class, spread-arse, on all future flights.

Inside the near-empty terminal, the sight of a public telephone fuelled a quick mood change. Walking happily past it, two thoughts struck. First, the years spent monitoring the detective inspector's acting style hadn't been in vain. Secondly, he might extend his California tour and call in at a film studio to show appreciative camera huggers there were more than just crocodile men from down under ready to strut their stuff for adoring film fans.

But before showing anything – licence for his rental car, smack supply or big-screen talents – to anyone, though, there was the small matter of attending to his full bladder. He looked around, spotted the Gents to his left and went in. Like the rest of the brightly lit terminal, this place was deserted as well. Nick relaxed, set his daypack down for the first time since leaving the island and got on with his reason for being there.

It surprised him then when the door squeaked open and an old man hobbled in and moved over to the washbasin. Seconds later, a thick-set bloke in jeans and a leather jacket, his head swallowed in a red beanie, entered and took up a position beside him. Nick tuned his ears in and listened. The bloke's need for being there couldn't be termed bladder-busting, and that's what aroused his suspicion. Nick's discomfort strengthened when a second rugby sized bloke arrived. He reached for a CLOSED FOR CLEANING sign, placed it outside, then snapped the lock in place and took up a waiting position behind him. Nick glanced around and gave everyone a poor smile. He was about to cut off midstream, when he suddenly caught sight of the old bloke clawing away at the side of his face. To his horror, that face stretched sideways, like it was auditioning for *Halloween III*, then ripped open and… Oh shit! Nick's stomach sank, his body went numb as Copper Harris's eyes fixed on him like a pair of headlights. Hands shot up under his arms, went behind his neck and pushed hard, banging his head into the wall. Jeeeessus. Not only that, but he was flat against the urinal pissing on his Reeboks.

He yelped in near-hysteria, 'You've got it wrong! It's Nick here! We're on the same team, remember?'

Copper Harris drew up close – wig in one hand, strips of latex in the other. His voice was ice. 'I don't recall a quick sale of the rescued smack supply being a part of the team's business plan, Nick.'

Panic-struck, Nick tried to think fast. 'No, no, no. Misunderstanding, mate. I was only doing a bit of market research, that's all. The gear's in the daypack, untouched. You can see for yourself.'

He heard the zip open and the faint tear of the plastic bag. Then there was just his thumping heartbeat before fingers, caked in powder, tapped at his lips.

'Taste it,' Copper Harris demanded.

Nick took some in on the end of his tongue and worked it around. It tasted like… 'Oh Jeeesus!'

'I hope he's there for you on the dark side, Nick, the genuine dark side.'

'Eastern side of Flinders Island, mate. A one-shack place called Patriarch Inlet. An old hermit named Pete lives there. That smack-head poacher and his girlfriend were there too.'

'You're dead,' Harris whispered in Nick's ear. 'You're just not buried yet.'

Nick squealed, 'I'll go back and get it! Now! And I won't take a cut! It's all yours, mate, as it should be after this stuff-up! I respect you too much…'

A hand slapped his mouth and nose, and stayed like a clamp.

'I like you too, Nick. But business is business.' Harris tasted every word. 'And when outcomes fail to meet expectations, it's time to turn in the keys and go for early retirement.'

The muscle-heads dragged Nick backwards. A noose dropped around his neck. Rope ran over metal. The noose tightened and lifted, biting into his flesh. His mouth snapped open. He bit into a finger, heard a scream and tried to match it with his own, but could only gag when his tongue got in the way.

*

While Bowman replaced the rented Beetle's knife-slashed tyres, Pete looked over at Jackson standing next to Constable Mitchell and said, 'If you want to take a walk with the constable – and for what it's worth, I think you should – then I'll stay here and keep an eye on things.'

'Were you able to get that medication for Ben?'

'Yes, with the help of the constable here. I'll take it up the road to him."

She thanked him and stepped down onto the sand.

Constable Mitchell followed. 'The thing is,' Mitchell said, a few minutes later, 'if I can't find out more about those slashed tyres, I'll have to consider contacting the big boys over on the mainland.'

Past the first lagoon, they sat down and looked out at a crayboat rolling on the swell, seagulls hovering in its wake.

'I've met Nick Jones twice,' Jackson said finally. 'I'll tell you about those meetings, and I'll give you what he came out here for but, before I do that, can I ask that my boyfriend be allowed to stay out here until he's better?'

'I don't have a problem with that, unless I receive instructions otherwise. I can't see that happening, though, in the short term, anyway.' He took a small notepad and biro from his shirt pocket and waited.

Jackson's eyes didn't shift from that crayboat until she'd told Constable Mitchell most of what had happened, keeping the most uncomfortable bits to herself. She finished off by saying, 'Nick Jones said he'd send those photos he took of Ben into the St Kilda police if he heard we'd informed.'

'Right. I'll deal with that.'

Only the crayboat's mast showed one moment, then it was King of Bass Strait the next.

'So let me get this straight. You say what this Nick Jones really left the island with was milk powder?'

'Yes.'

'Incredible. So where's the heroin now?'

'In a container under a bed in Pete's place.'

They spotted Pete walking along the beach towards them.

'That bloke with the missing little finger, can you describe him to me?'

'Big and broad, in his forties maybe. Deep voice. Short dark hair and a bushy beard.'

'Right.' Blind man, possible hit and run enforcer, hospital patient. It was that role of hospital patient that lingered in the constable's mind. How could anyone but a mole detective get access to a specific hospital bed? The question was, should he pursue it? Police corruption was big. Just the sort of size he wanted to keep away from. That's why he'd volunteered to come back here and take on this one-copper posting. Other than tracking down a cray poacher, or getting a stray cow back in its paddock, the closest he'd come to real police work was watching *The Bill* on Tuesday nights. And that's the way he wanted it to stay. So why not grab the heroin, ring the mainland, provide them with the basics and plead ignorance to anything more? Possible police corruption case closed. Well, from his end, anyway. And it was back to what he did best – the simple things: neighbourly duty by day, and home with the wife and baby daughter at night.

Pete arrived. He sat down next to Jackson, mentioning that Bowman had finished and was gone, and that he'd given the valium and glucodin to Ben. Then he went quiet again watching the crayboat.

The thing was, Mitchell thought moments later, once you started sticking your head in the sand, the position would only get more and more comfortable. So, what would it take to trace a Victorian coat and tie copper minus a small finger without word getting back to him? And this Nick bloke – comes for heroin and leaves with milk powder. Once he realises what he has, what chance would there be that he, or someone like him, would return to make amends? The constable's anxiety eased. Maybe there was an easier way to deal with this.

Walking back, Pete noticed the end of the road was empty of Beetles, including his own. Racing back to his shack, he went straight for the table where he kept his keys. They were gone. So was the money Nick Jones had dropped on the floor. Ten minutes later the three of them entered Bushed Out. Ben was gone.

'When does the last flight leave Whitemark for the day?' Pete asked the constable.

Mitchell checked his watch. 'Fifteen minutes ago.'

'If you'd be good enough to give me a ride to the airport, I'll pick up my car.'

*

Pete sat down on his rock, glanced over at his reclaimed Beetle at the end of road and said to Santi, 'Nothing happens, then everything seems to happen at once.'

'You reckon solitude's easier.'

He still tingled when she used words like 'reckon'. 'The past week it would've been, for sure.'

'Welcome back to the world.'

He sipped his tea and watched the ocean.

Santi's voice stayed close. 'You know, Pete, you've seen and talked to more people in the past few days than you have in the last two years. And though that Nick bloke came as a shock, as he would to anyone anywhere, the time spent with the girl, the few beers you've allowed yourself to have at the pub, the nattering sessions with Bowman, haven't appeared to set your comfort level back at all.'

'That heroin and the car episode didn't exactly serve as pacifiers.'

'No,' Santi agreed. 'But neither did Bridget Saunders knocking at the door that night, and the others who you were there for in the past. "It's what I do," I remember you saying from time to time up in Blackall.'

'Blackall was a different place in different times and circumstances.'

'Different in place and time, maybe so, but not in circumstance, Pete. What you did for Jackson you did for Bridget Saunders and the others. You settled them down. You helped them to take the next step.'

Pete saw that sea eagle again, skimming over the water. He followed it until it rose up suddenly and disappeared into the sun.

Having his full attention again, Santi continued, 'Perhaps it's time for you to take the next step.'

'Is it? And where would that lead me?'

For sounding interested, she rewarded him with a small smile that rimmed his eyes in tears. 'Back home you used to love searching out seafood recipes and surprising us with new dishes.' That it was rude to be direct with people was a legacy of her Indonesian upbringing. So she'd start on the periphery and work her way in, step by coercive step, until she arrived at the point she'd intended to make from the start. Such a time-consuming process, but an entertaining one too, he'd always thought. She went on, 'That little café and shop complex down from the hotel, the one that sells trinkets, shells and things.'

'What about it?'

Closing in on her target, her voice quickened. 'It's been up for lease or sale a long time now. Needs some work. They couldn't be asking much for it, could they?

'I don't know… I suppose not.'

'We've got money collecting dust in the bank now. So that part's covered. I reckon the only thing needed then, Pete, is attitude – yours. Not feeling too old and solitary to face up to the world again, to do something new.'

'Fill in the details for me.'

'It might sound fanciful.'

'I suspect it might, yes.'

'Pete's Seafood Restaurant and Souvenir Shop,' she burst out, her bright eyes engorged with the possibilities. She was in quick time mode now. 'Polish up that mountain of shells out back. Keep adding to it. Renovate the building. Open it just seasonally and on weekends maybe. Keep it simple. Only a few tables to start with, so there are no big costs once it's finished. You cook and employ one other person to handle the tables.' She slowed and went almost apologetic. 'Of course, it would mean buying a calendar, Pete, and keeping your eyes on the days again… Anyway, what do you reckon?'

'Fantasyland.' He rubbed a hand over his beard, before adding, 'at the moment,' as if the future could have some bearing on it.

16

Looking down at Flinders again only deepened his melancholy. Still too shocked and sore to think happy thoughts, Nick dwelled instead on the sudden disappearance of pain-free breathing, talking and eating from his list of life's most pleasurable activities. Hanging by a roped neck from the frame of a toilet cubicle, while being repeatedly hoisted and lowered back down onto piss-wet toes, could have that effect on anyone. But he still couldn't help taking the experience personally. His breathing was left shallow and wheezing. His once-resonant voice had fled its box, leaving behind a rasping, cough-like sound that scraped at his throat, like a swallowed sea urchin, whenever he tried to utter more than a few syllables. And the excruciating pain he'd felt when sampling a Big Mac meant he was off ingesting anything that couldn't be sucked through a straw.

And it wasn't just the pain inside his throat that raged either. The welts around his neck continued to itch and sting, despite abundant applications of the ointment he'd bought – along with a turtleneck skivvy, Akubra, new jeans, socks and sandshoes – while under strict supervision in the city.

But he had to admit all that was small news compared to the fact that he was still alive. Though for how long required further clarification. As the plane started to bank, he played back the first few minutes of his resurrection the previous day, starting with Harris's voice winging in from the void.

'Not conducive to best business practice is it, Nick, this attempt at going solo unannounced?'

'No.' *Geez, that hurt. The smell of urine was strong. His, he soon realised, looking down at his pant legs.*

'Hearing well, Nick?'

That seemed his only sense still working untroubled. He nodded to save his throat.

'Before leaving us, l just wanted to ask you some yes-no questions. Are you now feeling the need to reassess your priorities in life?'

Nick nodded.

'To put a greater emphasis on loyalty, on commitment to a higher power and working together for the common good?'

Nick nodded.

'Yes, I believe you. Got your credit card, Nick?'

He leaned to one side and pointed to his back pocket.

'Good boy.' Harris sat the container on Nick's lap. 'One day will be all you'll need. The next flight to Whitemark departs tomorrow at nine in the morning. Now that you're familiar with the taste of milk powder, you won't have any difficulty exchanging it for the smack down there, will you?' Harris didn't bother waiting for a response. 'The last flight arrives back here at six in the evening. Someone will be here to welcome you back. Of course, if you, or the item in question, are not on board, termination will be automatic and an appointment made with a funeral director of our choice. Now, if there are no further questions, why don't we help you up... That's it... Woaah!' Harris screwed up his nose and made a guttural sound. 'You missed the sandbox, Nick. We can't have you occupying prime St Kilda lodgings tonight reeking like this. After your ticket purchase, we'll get a bite to eat and buy some new clothes. No. Reverse that. We'll get the clothes first.'

'Flinders on the horizon,' the pilot parroted.

His voice pulled Nick's mind back. Yeah, yeah, yeah. He'd heard it too many times before. He knew what was next.

'Should have you steady on the ground in ten minutes.'

It was a pity this lacky-band airline didn't offer frequent-flyer points. Though, if they did, he was no certainty to be alive long enough to use them.

*

Jackson gave a quick laugh. 'It's beautiful,' she exclaimed, glancing down at what looked like a hairy bomb with legs cradled there in her arms.

She'd been reluctant to come, as she'd been reluctant to walk with him on the beach, but now she was pleased she was here. Baby-wombat therapy was starting to cool the anger she felt towards Ben, almost as much of a bastard in her eyes now as Nick was. Bye bye Ben, she whispered to the wombat staring trustingly back up at her. I hope there's a lifeline out there for you somewhere. She knew it would take time to get over him and the shock of what he'd turned into. But what was happening here was a good start, helped along by the fact that John, like Louise, knew nothing about the heroin, only that Nick and Ben were asking around for her.

'Did those two blokes find you,' John had asked her earlier.

She'd prepared for that question in advance. 'Yes. They came out yesterday,' she said, trusting that Constable Mitchell's request to Bowman and Pete – that nothing be said to anybody – would be strictly adhered to. Certainly, that wouldn't prove a problem for Pete. 'They were supposed to meet here and visit me as part of their tour of Tasmania, but got the dates mixed-up. They'll probably be doing an adult education course on calendar reading together next year. Anyway, they've left.' She felt there was justice in the fact that neither Ben nor Nick knew what really happened to the heroin. Anyway, it was well and truly over between her and first boyfriend Ben, wasn't it? It had been for weeks, probably longer.

John's face beamed as he took the baby wombat from her and began rocking it in his arms. 'I s'pose these would be all the rage for pet lovers up there in the big smoke where you come from.'

'Hardly.' She almost expected him to talk baby talk to the animal for the fuss he was making of it.

John deposited the wombat gently on the ground. It trailed closely behind them as they went into the weatherboard house, where John introduced her to his father, Rex.

He welcomed her and followed up by saying, 'It's good to see you right again.'

It took her a moment to realise that he was referring to her bicycle fall. That seemed weeks ago.

After she thanked him for helping her, John led her outside, past a hothouse 'full of tomatoes just screaming to be picked' and rows of fruit trees, before a three-legged dog hobbled up alongside the wombat.

'Red heeler.' John noted, as he got down to stroke the dog. 'Dad calls her Slowdog… She got bowled over a few months ago and was taken to Sam Healy, the vet I do holiday work for in Lady Barron. In a real mess she was. Its drought-hit owner said he couldn't afford to keep an invalid dog and suggested that Sam let her die, or push her along a bit. He might as well have asked Sam to put down one of his own grandchildren. Anyway, as I was down there at the time, Sam handed me a gown, explained the surgical instruments to me and just kept on talking away while he took off what was left of the dog's leg and blunted his stitching needle patching her up. While I was wheeling her out, Sam said, "She's done well to get this far. The next couple of hours should determine whether she survives or not." I told him that I had a magazine and that I wouldn't mind watching over her. Sam nodded and bumped up my holiday working hours after that.'

Jackson squatted down and ran her fingers over the many scars visible under the dog's short coat. As she did, its tail wagged into a blur. 'So how'd the dog get here?' she asked, thinking it was far from being a multiple-choice question, but wanting to hear him explain it.

'When I got down there the next day, the dog's tail was going at the same rate of knots it is now. She nearly took my fingers off when I offered her a bit of meat.' He grinned at the memory. 'Anyway, one or two things happened and a few days later I brought her home. She's not allowed in the paddocks, though. She could get hurt.'

Sure enough, after they entered a paddock, Slowdog turned and headed back towards the house.

Just the wombat followed now as they strolled past a dam and cows munching on fodder, before coming to an animal compound shaded by native trees at the back. Lying under them was the other wombat and the small wallaby – its hindquarters shaved around a crusty sore tinctured red in antiseptic. Jackson asked what had happened to it.

'There are islanders who call it "knocking down your dinner with a gun". But this one was lucky, the bullet missed its mark. Dad and I spotted it last week dragging its leg over the ground, so we managed to get a rope around it, and brought it back and I rang up Sam. Later on there was more surgery and non-stop instruction in our barn. Now I just have to stop any infection and keep him quiet. Too easy. He should be right to release in another week or so.'

When John opened the gate, the wombat rushed out and began pawing away at the ground.

'Now we can give both wombats some exercise.'

'They won't run away?'

John's face lit up again. He extracted a set of keys from his pocket. On the key ring was a silver medal he made a point of showing her. 'No chance of him escaping as long as I have this wombat magnet close by. Like super glue it is. Watch.' He lowered his arm as though the medal held an invisible lead, then turned and walked in a fast figure-eight pattern.

With their noses twitching like rabbits, the wombats followed right on his heel. When John stopped, they did too and stared up at him. The only thing the animals didn't mimic was the self satisfied grin on John's face.

'I might have to enter them in a sheep dog trial, what d'ya reckon?'

She suspected he was joking, but wasn't entirely sure. 'Are there magnets for other animals here as well?' she asked, digressing.

'Ah, maybe.' He went all wide-eyed and playful. 'To find out, you'll have to come back. A different day, a different animal, a different magnet.' He got down and stroked the wombats, and when Jackson's eyes turned to a nearby hill, he slipped slices of carrot into their mouths.

'Other than to the beach, do you take your wombats anywhere else?'

John followed her gaze. 'They enjoy lonely summits as much as lonely beaches, so I reckon where you're looking is where we should go.'

For half an hour they followed a stony track up past a bull barn and contorted gum trees to the hill's sloped summit. There they sat with their legs outstretched.

After a long silence, Jackson said, 'This might sound weird, but outside of an aeroplane, I can't remember ever being up this high before.'

'Major climbing expeditions aren't a regular feature for you in the big smoke, huh?'

'Beyond climbing over a fence, no, not a big feature.'

'Mount Strzelecki in the south is higher. We could climb that if you'd like.'

This time she put more thought into her answer. 'Maybe another time. We're both on the island to study, remember?'

'We could take our books.' He took a couple of carrots out of his pocket and passed them to her.

No sooner had he done that than the wombats closed in on her, their noses twitching.

Then it hit her. 'A different day, a different animal, a different carrot,' she noted, mimicking what he'd said to her earlier. She tossed the carrots on the ground. 'Magnets come in many different shapes and colours, don't they?'

'You've noticed.'

'I'd have to be blind not to.' She shook her head in mock disappointment.

'Still smiling?' he asked.

Yes, she was, and it surprised her. 'I'm learning to,' was what she said.

'Good. It's called wombat therapy, and it's yours prescription-free.'

Their wombat thoughts seemed to match then. A crow cawed nearby.

'Do you come up here much?' she asked.

'I used to, when I felt the need to get away from things.'

She eyed him curiously. 'What things could you possibly get away from up here that you couldn't down there?'

He reached for the carrot nubs and tossed them down the hill. Their meals interrupted, the wombats scampered after them.

'Screaming, crying, throwing things. My mother's mostly. But that ended six years ago when she took off to Sydney and never came back.'

This was a topic she *did* know about. 'Do you stay in contact with her?'

'I do now. She writes from a place called Marrickville. I write back.

She's with somebody up there now and seems happy enough. She's asked me to come up and stay with her, but I haven't as yet.'

'Because you're bitter about what happened?'

'No, it's not that. Mum always wanted to go to the mainland to sample life on a bigger scale. She was born on the island and started going with Dad after she finished high school here. A year later she got pregnant with me. So for her, that meant marrying a man whose world was made up of what you can see from here and from the hotel in Whitemark... No, there's no bitterness. It's just that I've never been anywhere else but Launceston. Even there I think how little I understand things away from Flinders. Grunge and rap music sound like cats fighting to me. Harley Davidsons and Ducati sports bikes are a bit flash for paddock work. And all I know about tattoos and nose rings is that they're restricted to cattle here. Why I do feel so good about this place is what I know about. Everything that swims, slides, flies and walks in animal form around here, people on Flinders want to know about too.' His words gained pace and intensity. 'And by sharing their interests, I'm sharing their feelings about things. I've got a place here, a job to do. True, it's not the sort of job that'll buy yachts and build mansions on Sydney Harbour, but it will keep me connected to what's really important in my life.'

'It's good to know where you belong.'

'Yeah, it is.' He took a moment to wind down. 'Anyway, you should know I get a bit carried away by things I feel strongly about. Sorry.'

'Don't be.'

'I can bore people silly talking about Flinders.'

'Not me.'

His gaze stayed on her for a while. 'So how long do you think you'll be studying down there next to the Sandman?'

Her eyes met his, pointedly. 'Pete, you mean?'

'Yeah, I do. Like him, stay on the island long enough – even in a place as remote as his – and you'll earn yourself a nickname.'

He dropped his eyes in the hazy direction of Patriarch Inlet. 'He's a good bloke, the Sandman.'

'I know.' For two seconds, tears sprang to her eyes. She blinked them away. 'I guess I could stay another four or five days. Certainly I'll be out of there before I've earned the name Sandgirl.' The conversation had turned. She was the focus now and she wasn't comfortable with that.'Anyway, the books are calling. I'm going to have to get back.' She stood up, thanking him. It occurred to her that she'd been doing a lot of that lately.

'A pleasure. It's been good…really good.'

He and the wombats stayed close to her all the way down the hill.

17

The old fossil was the key. So spotting him sitting up on a rock like old King Neptune was a big bonus. There was only his Vee-dub at the end of the road now, with new tyres to replace the ones knife-tested and found wanting. Nick's eyes lingered on that car and a wave of nostalgia swept through him as he reflected on the good old days here just two days earlier. He'd been a man with a master plan for wealth and influence then. Now look at him.

Needing to work through his depression, Nick lowered his binoculars, took off his Akubra and aviator sunnies, and checked that his shoulder pads and black moustache were still in place. After parking his Bowman Beetle in bush half a kilometre down the road, it had been hot, throat-challenging work scrub bashing out here on such a muggy day. Still, not a lot of energy would be needed for what lay ahead. The old man was hardly a physical match-up for Arnold Schwarzenegger and, once he was taken care of, Nick could use the road getting back to the car.

It took Nick an anxiety-filled minute to wrap the rope and noose around his right shoulder, rock-climber-style, before scampering out of the trees and over sand to the headland rocks along the shoreline. He scaled them and edged his way along until he was behind the old man, posing there with his eyes on the water like he was in a photo-shoot for *Contentment Homes* magazine.

Nick transferred the rope to his hand and checked that no one else was about, before moving stealthily past the open door to the old man and dropping the noose around his neck. His recent memories about this weren't good.

'Three things,' he snapped too forcefully, jerking Pete up. In pain, he rasped, 'Don't scream. Don't bullshit me. And do what I say. Understand?' He wished he'd written up cue cards. 'The smack supply. Inside or outside?'

'Welcome back to the world,' Santi had said. And that's what flashed through Pete's mind before he answered, 'Inside, under the bed.'

How surprising, Nick thought. 'Let's get it. Turn around and I'll decap…' Nick grimaced and lowered his voice to a murmur. 'Just get it.'

Pete handed over the daypack and Nick took the plastic bag out, examining it very closely. What looked to be a thin film of powder lay at the top. He licked it. It didn't taste like milk, but with what his taste buds had endured recently, he wasn't putting much trust in them. 'Smack this time?'

'I've no doubt it is,' Pete answered, nodding. Strange how calm he felt. There was another way this could go. Though it was a huge long shot, Pete still wanted to explore the possibility of talking this out. 'The kettle's hot. Care for a drink? Coffee and tea are on the sink. I'll stay here on the bed.'

A drink of any sort was tempting. But… 'Piss off, old man. This is hardly a social call. Are your boarders around?'

Boarders? There was no sense correcting him. 'No, they're gone.' This was only going to go one way – Nick's. A pity, because he was obviously here at the behest of Mr Big. And if things went according to plan, returning to St Kilda with the payload was only going to cause Nick considerably more pain, and perhaps worse.

Nick dropped the bag back in and zipped up the daypack. 'Sit down at the table. Hands behind you, feet under the chair.' He tightened the noose around Pete's neck and tied off his hands and feet, before pausing to think. He hadn't entered the detective inspector's league yet, had he? He hadn't actually killed anyone, or been immediately responsible for anyone's death – well, not that he was aware of anyway. Though true, that car park shooter had joined the ranks of the road-killed, but he was in the passenger seat when that happened, not behind the wheel.

Seconds later, Nick decided to loosen the rope around the old man's feet. By taking little bird steps, he'd be able to get out to the main road in a matter of hours. While it wouldn't do a lot for his arthritis, at least he wouldn't be found as a skeleton here.

Nick went to the sink, poured himself a glass of water and peeked out the window. Satisfied with the emptiness out there, he left quickly.

Two minutes later, Constable Mitchell burst in through the back door. 'Okay?' he blurted out, moving to free Pete.

'Fine,' Pete answered softly. 'Though I don't think the same could be said for our Nick Jones. He's lost confidence and turned his volume control down.'

'From what you said earlier, I thought his voice would attract passing ships out there. I could barely hear him.'

Two other men in jeans and navy blue jumpers came in through the same door. One carried what looked to be a miniature laptop in his hands. He set it down on the table and studied the screen for a moment before pressing a button. A faint beeping noise started.

'All systems go?' the constable asked him.

'Uh huh,' the man muttered, engrossed in what he was watching.

'That's it, apparently, along with what's sewn in the daypack,' the constable said to Pete as Jackson appeared, standing at the back doorway. 'Surveillance will never be the same again,' the constable continued, his voice turning heavy with irony. 'What we're witnessing is an auspicious moment in the island's history. The first time a satellite tracking device has been used here to fight the ravages of crime.'

18

Sitting next to him in the airport's waiting room, Jackson recalled the other places she'd been with Pete the past week. The hotel lounge bar and outside his shack. On Bushed Out's veranda when the constable said the 'sting' operation had worked and, besides Nick, another man had been nabbed, although the constable couldn't divulge the details. And again today in his Beetle going into town, then here. Jackson suspected their long, shared silences together had been as important as their talks in making them so comfortable in each other's company. Certainly the silences had occupied more time.

'I was just thinking how long it's been since I was in here,' Pete said, eventually. 'I came in winter, so more than two years ago. Nothing seems to have changed.'

She considered how they'd only ever talked about her and the problems she'd brought with her to the island, one big one in particular. The three photos on his wall flashed into her mind.

'Where were you before you came to Flinders?'

He took a moment to answer. 'Queensland.'

'Great place, I hear.'

'I've heard people say that too.' As they stared out the window at the twin-engine plane, both were aware a certain crossroads had been reached. Where this last chat would go – if anywhere – was up to him now.

'My wife and two boys were killed in a car accident up there,' he said, half a minute later. 'So I came here needing the remoteness…and the ocean.'

It saddened but didn't shock her. And she felt complimented that he'd provided her with the key to who he was out at Patriarch Inlet; a key she felt certain no one else on the island had. It seemed to balance things up between them. Ironic, wasn't it? How people often got closer just before they were due to part.

'How did it happen?'

He kept his eyes on the plane, and his voice was deep and confiding as he told her about his family's annual holiday. As he did, he could still hear the synchronous 'thump, thump, thump' of funk music blaring away in the back seat, and his boys shrieking and sit dancing in accompaniment all the way to the Gold Coast. There they always stayed in the same thirteenth floor Ocean Royale apartment with its views of the open sky and ocean on one side, and condominiums and green hills on the other. He and his wife had honeymooned there just after the place was built; and being a couple well-accustomed to the diary-dictated routines of life, plans for renewing their July honeymoon at the Gold Coast had never been questioned. It was 'the complete break untuk liburan yang selalu hebat!' Santi eagerly reminded him in her mixture of English and Indonesian. Not that it was ever necessary to.

Just as Pete started to translate Santi's Indonesian for Jackson, the pilot breezed through.

'The flight's delayed a few minutes,' he said, interrupting. 'I'll give you a five-minute warning bell when we're ready to go.' They nodded and let a minute of that time pass in silence before Jackson gave Pete a smile.

'I'll get to the Gold Coast one day,' she said, trying to nudge him along.

His mind backtracked again.

Santi was pressed against him in bed, Her long fingers stroking his chest after they'd made love. 'Go to the principals' conference in Townsville, Pete,' she said, in that languorous way of hers.

It was here, with what she said, that he resumed his story.

'Then fly down to the Gold Coast after it's over,' Santi continued. 'Don't worry about us getting there. John can help with the driving. We'll be right.'

So off he went and, after flying down to meet them, he waited a day and a half for their knock on the door, too anxious to leave the unit for long. He was watching the weather report that talked about heavy outback rain when the knock finally came. He raced to the fridge. Popped, the champagne cork nearly holed the roof He dashed to the door, swept it open and… 'The complete break…' was how she'd put it. And it was that that rang in his ears when he saw those two plain-clothes officers standing in the doorway. One held up his identification.

He must have asked them in, for they sat on the lounge suite across from him, leaning forward, their big hands clasped together.

Ten years older than Santi, he'd always assumed he'd be the first to go. 'Accident?' he heard himself ask, horrified, but wanting to dispense with the preliminaries.

'Uh huh,' they chorused softly.

He trembled. 'Which one?' he muttered weakly, desperate to hear the name of a hospital, a diagnosis, prognosis, and knowing the next few seconds would determine everything.

Their hands unclasped, then clasped again. Their faces stayed frozen, their silence serving as words.

'The lot,' he muttered. It was a statement, not a question.

The one on the right nodded, while the other one found his voice and started to explain. 'Heavy rain between Blackall and Charleville…'

All that emptiness all at once. The room reeled. It was like their voices were riding a merry-go-round – close one moment, distant the next.

'… A speeding road train hit the back of the car your son was driving and sent it careering off the road into the scrub,' the policeman said.

Pete went quiet now, the shutter on his memory dropping. He glanced around at Jackson, who was sitting perfectly still facing him, her eyes large and wet. 'So Flinders,' he said as a postscript, smiling ruefully.

'Boarding in five minutes,' the pilot called out from the door, breaking the quiet.

Pete stood up when Jackson did. The focus turned to her again.

'Anyway, the end of an eventful week,' Pete said. 'Enough intrigue to last lifetimes. And now, on a more positive note, there's the challenge of VCE exams, university entry decisions to be made, a holiday job to devote yourself to.'

'That last one's no certainty,' she said, not yet recovered from what she'd just been told. 'I had to quit at Burger King to get the time off to come here.'

'Oh.' He glanced around the terminal, before settling his eyes back on her. 'That café we were in this morning, what did you think of it?'

The jump in conversation surprised her. 'It was okay. It could use a bit of work and a coat of paint, though.'

'It could, yes.' They stepped aside for three passengers heading out the door. 'The café's for sale and I'm thinking about buying it.' He paused to gauge her reaction. 'The thought of doing that surprises me too. Something about taking a step, a small one, anyway, back into the world. I've always fancied myself as a seafood cook, though you wouldn't know it from the fish I cook up in the mornings. However, if I do take the place on, I'll need to get some renovations done and have it ready for the tourist trade in January. Then I'll need to employ someone who's reliable, experienced and customer-friendly to handle the tables. The thing is, I've only met one person here who I know would be right for the job.' He took a scrap of paper from his shirt pocket and handed it to her. 'My address is there. While you were in at the hotel, I went over to the post office and rented myself a postbox. Within the next month or so, would you let me know if you'd be willing to return to Flinders and work for me over the summer holidays? Only if it turns out to be convenient for you, of course.'

Jackson nodded, stunned; but before she could say anything, Louise's voice blared out across the terminal, 'I knew I'd make it.' She drew up close and kissed and hugged her niece. 'Why Island Air continues to print precise departure and arrival times on their timetables, without adding "although we're usually running thirty minutes late", is a mystery to me.' She glanced at Pete. 'Hello.'

'Hello.'

Jackson picked up where Louise left off. 'Well, things are improving, auntie. My flight's only running fifteen minutes late, and the warning bell's sounded, so I've got to go.'

'Okay. That suits, actually. I've got Tagger minding the bar. I stay too long here and he'll start swallowing the profits.' Jackson smiled at that. 'Thank you for what you've done for me.' She kissed her aunt's cheek.

'What I've had the opportunity to do for you, dear, is next to nothing.'

'It was enough.' Jackson glanced over at Pete and thanked him too before adding, 'I'll write about the holidays, okay?'

He nodded and Jackson left smiling, but not entirely dry-eyed.

Watching Jackson get on the plane, Louise asked, 'Pete, isn't it?'

'Pete, yes.'

She turned to him. 'I'd like to thank you too, Pete.'

'You already have. At the hotel.'

'For being there when she came off the bike, yes.' Louise paused to study him for a moment. 'I might explain to you that, in the absence of a local counselling service, and invariably lightened by the salve of a few drinks, hotel patrons here air confidences over the front bar that wouldn't find a comfortable hearing anywhere else on the island. Husbands, behind all their bravado, having a close look at themselves and not liking what they see. Wives, suffering from island fever, in a quandary about what to do about it. I don't have any certificates or counselling books, Pete, but what I have got is years of watching and listening experience. So this past week my highly sociable niece drops in claiming to be seeking total isolation. Then two suspicious types breeze in asking around for her. Then Bowman fobs me off about a flattened tyre outbreak and the local copper starts boycotting the hotel. And finally, to top it all off, a long-time resident refugee from life suddenly feels comfortable enough with humanity to provide my niece with a taxi service to the airport.' She furrowed her brow and gave him an inquisitive look. 'Being an interested spectator to all this, I've been asking myself what's going on.'

'Understandably.'

Her eyes stayed fastened on him. 'But you're not going to enlighten me, are you?'

'No.'

'So I'm left to draw my own conclusions.' She broke eye contact finally and looked around the airport. 'Okay, I will. But one thing I won't have to speculate on is Jackson's frame of mind when she left here just now. It was heaps better than when she arrived. And I'd venture to say that here on Hinders, anyway, only you and my two former confidants – Bowman and the constable – know why.' Her eyes found him again. 'Though in not saying anything to anyone, you three are obviously protecting her. And from whatever it is you're protecting her from, I'm truly thankful. And to show my appreciation, I'd like to borrow another hour of your solitude time now and shout you lunch at the café.'

'I thought someone named Tagger was swallowing up the profits.'

'For every negative, there's a positive. I'm hungry. As well, I'm curious to know what my niece is thinking about doing over the Christmas holidays, and why you were browsing around our upcoming lunch site this morning. You will at least share those two bits of information with me, won't you?'

19

Harris poured himself another glass of Grange Hermitage wine and gazed out over the abyss. 'As I recall, Nick, we were discussing retirement when last we were together. Have you come up with any more ideas about the topic since then?' He waited a moment. 'I've never known you to be so quiet.'

As Nick was bound, gagged and hooded, Harris decided to push the conversation along on his own. 'Actually, I've had the time to research the topic lately.' He sipped his wine, savouring its taste. 'Did you know, Nick, that on average sheilas live seven years longer than us blokes. And the reasons for that read like a "What's what in old fart ailments". Heart, kidney and liver disease, prostate cancer, diabetes, brain cell displacement.'

Harris gave Nick a contemptuous look. 'Judging by the state you're in at the moment, you could be thinking longevity is vastly over-rated. But for those of us who don't, what do you think we should do to improve our senior citizen prospects?'

He glanced at Gutbuster and Big Butch – his two minders standing on either side of Nick – to see if answers were forthcoming from them. When they just shrugged and stared at the ground, Harris continued. 'One answer is to retain a purpose in life and don't retire. Or, as in my case, if a situation develops where voluntary retirement is no longer on the option board, sign the papers and continue on as though nothing's changed.'

He gulped his wine down and poured himself another one. "As a Bloke, Living To Be A Hundred Before Entering Full Retirement" will be the title of my autobiography when I am and I do. I've got the title for the first chapter on going global in my head already – "Business Acumen in the Global Drug Economy". Acumen, Nick. Meaning knowledge that strengthens with age. It's a word that's lost on you.'

He held his refill up to the sun and concentrated on its colour, then swished it around in his glass and sampled it. 'Anyway – and you'll notice how I'm forced to use the first person singular here – take my business, for instance. It's locally based and extremely sensitive to the introduction of new products, market fluctuations and the necessity to downsize staff. So what to do?'

He didn't bother looking around this time. 'Broaden the business base – diversify. Without that you go stale. Go stale and you lose your grip. Lose your grip and you're worms' meat. It's a lesson for us all.' He laughed thickly at something only he knew about, then emptied his glass and topped it up again.

'You know, Nick, I've got an eye for where all this going global is headed.' He kept his two eyes on the abyss. 'I can see it in the banners waving – "Academia Swamped by the Tidal Wave of Market Forces". And in the dusty highbrow set throwing open their curtains and taking in the light of the new millennium. In universities dropping Shakespeare for Drug Cartel Studies, establishing Global Drug Economy professorships, lecturing positions and degrees. Between the two of us, Nick,' he said as a friendly aside, 'I could get used to wearing an academic gown. So, what I'm saying is you'd have to be bent as a scrub tick to give up on the additive business in these blue-chip times, wouldn't you?' All that magnificent space out there continued to draw up visions for Harris.

'But not just yet. There's still the matter of stamping "paid back" on the file of that nowhere hermit and his boarders you were spouting off about earlier. It'll be the last, nostalgia-filled item of business dating back to my drug squad and crime stopper days. No rush, though. I'll let the dust settle first.' He drank to that before breathing in audibly through his nose and exhaling.

'Ah, this Snowy Mountain air. It certainly beats what's circulating around in the boot of the car, wouldn't you agree?' He poured himself the remnants of the bottle and looked over at the car trying to decide whether he should open up another one. He decided against it.

'Going solo, Nick, then grabbing milk powder instead of smack, then being charged, summonsed to appear and having to be bailed by a team member. Ever heard of the term "three strikes and you're out"? I believe it's been popularised by our American cousins. Well, at least you won't have to worry about appearing.'

He looked over the edge for any hang gliders or rock climbers. None that he could see down there. Just the gorge sliding into shadow far below. 'It's what I plan to do in the future, Nick. Get outdoors more. Experience this country's remote places, its pristine wilderness.'

He nodded to the two minders, who tossed Nick off the cliff.

Watching him disappear, Harris added one last thought, 'Downsizing, Nick. The inevitable result of poor performance outcomes.'

20

December

Though her mother would no doubt disagree, Jackson felt she was too old to be snooping around the Christmas tree seeing what presents were under it for her. But she snooped around anyway. This year, in addition to the threadbare stocking her mother was never going to stop filling up for her, there were three big presents from Santa Claus, two from her mother and, for the first time, one from David. It was soft, rectangular and wrapped in bright red paper. It had to be some sort of clothing item – like a blouse or light jumper. Probably custom-made and purchased exclusively through the Mazda MX5 Owners' Ezibuy Program. She smiled. Something told her she'd like it.

She'd have to give him a present in return. Perhaps a wine rack with MX5s engraved all over it, though he probably had one. A box of chocolates looked the more likely option. Nothing yet from her father, not that it would fit under the tree anyway. Big enough to slow the 747 transporting it down to Melbourne, the package always arrived late. No such problems sending up his box of chocolates, though, nor arranging the delivery of his roses. She'd done both the previous day.

Roses weren't what daughters-adopted or otherwise – were supposed to give their fathers. But all she knew is that on a whim she'd had them delivered that first Christmas after he'd left. A week later he rang and they talked for almost an hour about things that were happening in her life. And every year since then he'd done the same. Like her mother's Christmas stocking, his annual phone call – prompted by red roses, guilt or whatever – was something she wanted to go on forever. She'd thought long and hard about this. It had something to do with retaining the shared joy of that first stocking and past Christmases together. It was about feelings for people standing up to the effects of time and changed circumstances (like divorce), of making gestures of affection time-proof. Ah, wax on, Lady Shakespeare, she chided herself. Off with the fairies at the bottom of the garden again, as was her habit this time of the year.

Her thoughts turned to Pete. She'd sent him a Christmas card with a note saying how much she was looking forward to working for him in a couple of weeks' time, if he hadn't changed his mind, or employed someone else. She wondered if he'd be getting anything else over Christmas.

The phone rang. Still season-struck, she went over and lifted the receiver. While the phone beeped away, she wondered if her father was ringing up early. If so, for the first time ever, certain things would have to be censored from their conversation. 'Christmas-in-waiting, Jackson speaking.'

'That satin voice. Still a bit on the husky side, still guaranteed to recharge dormant heartstrings. I ask myself regularly, Jack, how I've been able to wait so long before hearing it again.'

Christmas feelings evaporated. Her mood plummeted. 'Could it have something to do with you stealing money and an old man's car and leaving me island-stranded to sort out the police response?' With huge help from Pete and the constable, she'd been able to do that, hadn't she? So stuff him. There was no way he'd be getting the straight story out of her. That story, like their relationship, was over – dead in the Patriarch water.

Her voice thickened with anger. 'I've been waiting too, Ben – waiting for an explanation!'

His voice took on a repentant tone. 'Thanks for what you did for me, Jack. No one else would have done the same. And…well, merry Christmas.'

'Where are you?'

'Somewhere I'm certain you've never been.'

'Besides Melbourne and Flinders Island, that's everywhere. Try narrowing it down for me.'

'I'm sorry, Jack.'

'Sorry for what you've done or sorry for not telling me where you are?'

'Both.'

Her sigh was loud and exasperated. 'Ben, the police aren't guarding the place. No one's over my shoulder listening in. The phone's not being bugged.'

'You might not know that. Have you been reading the news papers lately?'

'Yeah. People are dying in Iraq.'

'There's a bit of that happening on the streets of Melbourne too. Gangland warfare, big street names stopping bullets while watching their kids playing Saturday sport. A couple of the names have been familiar to me.'

'Really? So you've rung up to hear my so-called satin voice and give me a briefing on the latest gangland murders and…and to apologise. Well, thanks for that. Has it been worth the obvious big effort for you?'

'I'm sorry, Jack.'

'Your vocabulary has shrunk, Ben. What's the problem? Has heroin-related Alzheimer's set in?'

'No, no heroin. Even the beer's being rationed.'

Her anger eased a little. 'Good… I'm pleased to hear that.' And she was. An awkward silence grew between them.

'Have you got any plans for the holidays?' he asked finally.

'Travelling. Though not to somewhere I've never been before.'

'To do what?'

'Do you want me to tell you first what it's not to do with?'

'Not particularly.'

Her sigh was softer this time. 'Waiting on tables at a restaurant in Whitemark.'

'Right… Money good?'

'I don't know yet, but I do know the people I'll be mixing with will be.'

'Great. Good luck with it. Listen, I've gotta go. I'll be in touch.

And please know how much I'm missing you and that it has been worth the effort ringing, and *will* be again. I'll make it all up to you soon. Promise.'

'Hang up, Ben. The phone buggers are about to work out where you're ringing from.'

21

Early January

Jackson heard the female singer's voice from a shack she barely recognised now.

> To you, I would give the world
> To you, I'd never be cold
> Cuz' I feel that when I'm with you
> It's all right
> I know it's right...

Her eyes wandered over the sea – its drowsy swells setting the tempo for the song.

> And the songbirds keep singing that they know the score
> And I love you
> I love you
> I love you
> Like never before...

From out of the trees, a small brown and white dog scampered stiff-legged up to her. It looked like a clone of the three-legged one John had shown her at his place two months earlier. Tail wagging, and whimpering its greetings, the dog gave her an acceptance sniff, then led her on.

She spotted Pete studying trellised tomatoes in a new glass hothouse next to his newly painted shack.

When he turned her way, his face lit up and he hurried out. 'Jackson!' Having got within arms' distance, he was suddenly unsure how to physically greet her. He settled for clasping her hands in his and shaking them. 'It's so good to see you.'

Her smile matched his. 'Watching over dogs and vegies now instead of drug runners, huh Pete?' Blunt maybe, but it was important that everything between them was above board.

Pete chuckled, freeing her hands. He'd had plenty of experience in dealing with double-ended statements. He knew which end to ignore. 'Yes. Going for more variety in my life nowadays.'

'I like your taste in music.'

His smile waned. 'Eva Cassidy. She was Santi's favourite singer. Mine too, if the truth be known. We used to dance to her *Songbird*.'

No hidden topics for him either, Jackson thought, strangely touched by his immediate openness. They were quickly back where they'd left off at the airport.

Pete's voice brightened. 'Anyway, less of me and more of you. How'd the exams go?'

'Okay.'

'How much okay?'

She couldn't help grinning. 'Okay enough to scrape into Monash. Education, English and Art to start.'

'Oh, Jackson. You're into teaching then. That's terrific!'

Her eyes moistened suddenly, and she had no idea why. She looked away. 'The place looks great.' In the time it took to say that, she went dry-eyed again.

'Coming from a person who's had so much experience with local shacks, that means a lot. C'mon, I'll show you the farm.'

Besides the trellised tomatoes in the hothouse, there were cucumbers, poles wrapped in runner beans, beds of lettuce and silver beet, broccoli and carrots 'just screaming to be picked', to quote another local primary producer.

Back outside, Pete bent down and gave his grateful dog a pat. 'Its owner died just after you left. Rex brought her out, but she soon went bush looking for what she had before. No unusual around here, is it? Anyway, she came back after a few days, obviously thinking this place would do.' He scratched the dog's ears while talking to it. 'We've got a few things in common, haven't we, old girl? Same sleeping habits. Same interest in walks and vantage points in the sun.'

Passing through the shack's open door, Pete went over and turned off Eva Cassidy. 'Recognise the place?' he asked, turning back round.

'Barely.'

A solar panel and skylight were on the roof. Enlarged windows brought more of the outdoors in. Dark carpet covered the floor. There were matching curtains, new cupboards and potted plants on the sink. His pine-framed sketches supplemented the photos of his family on the walls.

Jackson took a bunch of cellophane-wrapped aster daisies out of her daypack and handed them to him. 'Fully imported from Melbourne,' she said, her small smile bolstered by memory. 'You might recognise the daypack?'

'I do, yes.' The irony in what it was being used for now wasn't lost on him. He accepted the flowers, thanking her. 'They'll be the feature of our luncheon,' he said, reaching to get a glass jar from the cupboard.

'I've brought along a vase as well.' She got that out too and half filled it with water from the jug. She took the flowers from him, unwrapped them and placed them in the vase on middle of the table.

'Magnificent.' The flowers held his gaze. 'Santi always loved her flowers in vases.'

And just like that, it happened again – another instant eyewash. She turned away and looked at their wedding photo, while counting silently in French.

'Anyway, I hope you're hungry. I've got enough fish to feed half the island.' Pete offered her the choice of stoking up the stove and cooking, or salad making and drink preparation.

'Stove and cooking, thanks,' she said, turning. She noticed three place settings on the table. 'Is the dog eating with us, or have you taken in a boarder?'

For just a moment, Pete recalled when he last heard that word 'boarder' used. 'John's coming with some seedlings. He'll be joining us.'

'Oh.' That pleased her and her smile told him so.

They went about their chores in familiar silence. When they heard the sound of a vehicle coming in, Pete went to the fridge, pulled out a bottle of wine and began reading its label, or pretending to, anyway. 'Best opened next to a vase of imported aster daisies, this Flinders Island Chardonnay has lovely melon and peach fruit overtones with lifted fruit aromas and spicy vanillin oak. Sip it with Patriarch Inlet trevally smothered in home-grown tomatoes and pan-fried on a wood stove.' He reached around her and tossed a slice of tomato on the fish in the pan. 'We've obviously got the right wine here.'

She eyed him, smiling. Her expectations of what she'd be returning to here were in tatters. Shack renovation, glasshouse vegies, orphaned dog companion, Eva Cassidy and bottles of wine. That small step back into the world – well, the minuscule Flinders Island part of it anyway – had turned into a big step that had cheered and energised him. 'Are you making your own wines nowadays too, Pete?'

'No, just the labels. But I might talk to John today about getting some vines.' From the tight-lipped grin on his face, she doubted he would. 'Care for a drop of this, or would you prefer a fully imported beer from the mainland?' His grin widened. 'There's tea in the pot also,' he added.

'I think I'll try something with melon and peach…whatever.'

'Good. I'll join you.'

John tapped on the door and entered carrying a small cardboard box. He beamed a smile and his eyes went straight for her. 'Hi. I saw the extra Vee-dub out there with the P-plates, and it took a minute for me to work out who belonged to it. Signed off on bicycles now, have you?'

'Thankfully… How'd your exams go?'

'Okay. Yours?'

'Distinctions,' Pete interrupted, handing John a stubby. Despite Jackson denying those results, he added, 'She's on her way to Monash to become a teacher, aren't you, Jackson?' That note of pride again in his voice.

She let a few seconds pass. 'Yes, Monash,' she said quietly, down playing the announcement. I'll just see how things go.'

'Things'll go well. You're too bright and determined for them not to. Anyway, have a seat at the table here, John, and tell us what you've brought.'

John sat down eagerly. 'A dozen lettuce seedlings and a couple of dozen tomato seedlings. The tommies should fruit until winter in the hothouse.'

Food was served up as they talked about the long growing season. Then, while it lounged in a block of sunlight on the floor, the dog was the topic of conversation before Pete filled up the glasses and went to the fridge for another stubby for John.

When Jackson asked if the opening date for Pete's Seafood Restaurant was still the same, Pete glared over at John and said, 'The date's the same, but there's been some debate about the name of the place. You'll have to direct any further queries to John here.'

Now it was Jackson's turn to glare at John. 'Well?'

His smiled lengthened. 'The Sandman's.'

'Yes! I like it!'

Pete's response was less enthusiastic. 'Since you're going to be a big part it, I suppose it's opportune that you do.' Looking over at John, he blew out an exaggerated sigh. 'Voted down, aren't I?' His voice lightened in resignation. 'Well then, perhaps it's time to make the name official. I've got a fine bottle of red…'

'Not for me,' Jackson piped up, already feeling the effects of what she'd had. 'What's in my glass is enough.'

'Understandable. Though I thought I might share a bit with John. I've started a small cellar under the shack. I'll just go and grab a bottle. Be right back.'

The dog rose and followed him out.

'Great fish,' John said, moments later.

'Thanks. Nothing special.'

'Maybe you should do the cooking at The Sandman's and let Pete handle the customers.'

'Up to today, I thought he'd be the last one on the island to willingly do that.'

'Yeah. Well, he's been getting about a bit more lately. He shares the occasional beer with my father and his mate, Tagger, and in doing that he gains entry into the social set nattering over the bar to Louise. That's not to say he's ready to head up the Patriarch Inlet Tourist Council yet.'

'I thought that job had already been taken.'

He grinned at the floor. 'Only at selected times…for selected people.'

Pete ducked his head in. 'The dog's taken off. I'll have to go after her.'

'Need help?' John asked, hopping up.

'No, no. If you get restless, the dishes will need a going over, or you might want to walk off the lunch. Back soon.'

Feeling very mellow with the way things were at the moment, Jackson finished her wine and took her dishes to the sink. While John took a bucket out to the water tank, she stared out the window at the sea.

John came back in and reached around her, squeezing in some detergent and filling the sink with water.

Her eyes didn't budge the entire time he did that. 'It's the emptiness, you know, John,' she said, starting to wash up. 'Of nothing else being out there but ocean and sand, birds and the sky. I've missed it and I never thought I would.'

He grabbed the tea towel off the hook. 'What about my wombats? Did you miss them too?'

'Of course. Rarely did a day go by when I didn't ache to see them again, and their magnets.'

He chuckled. 'Both are still around. Which is more than can be said for some of the things that were once a part of this place.'

'I know. About all I recognised was the furniture and Pete's family on the wall.'

'His family? Are they? Where?'

She turned, surprised he didn't know, and pointed to them.

After viewing the photos close up, John came back and said, 'Where are they now?'

While Jackson hesitated, wondering if telling him would breach Pete's trust, John asked, 'Dead?'

She felt torn, but nodded quickly. 'Don't tell him I said anything.'

'Of course not.'

'The three of them were killed in a Queensland car accident while Pete was away at a conference.' She spared him the details.

'So that's why he came out here. Dad and I thought something like that had happened.'

Silence took over. She washed and he dried.

'Right,' John exclaimed, after everything had been put away. 'I think a regulation, fire-up the memory walk is in order.'

'Tourist Council's open for business, is it?' It felt good being back on lighter ground again. 'Got your wombats?'

'Two, tied to the back of the flat-tray. Come on, they've missed you.'

Sitting propped up against a tree trunk, Pete watched them leave. He stroked his dog curled up next to him and said, 'Clear as a bug on a bald head.'

Santi's voice was close. 'It was with us too.'

'From that first day di rumah makan di Yogyakarta. You and your girl friend at one table, saya-sebagai seorang turis-duduk di meja yang dekat. The old trick – I ask you for directions to the Sultan's palace having no intention whatsoever of going there while you remained so close.'

'Meeting you then, cintaku, affected my plans too.'

There'd be no shifting the heavy knot of sadness Pete carried around with him. He knew that. But on the margins of his life now there were everyday things happening and people who'd become important to him again. He kept his eyes on Jackson and John, and continued talking to Santi.

22

Jackson checked her watch: eight o'clock. The place was empty except for a Queensland couple celebrating their twentieth wedding anniversary, and a burly man in fishermen's gear and wearing a red beanie, like an egg cosy, halfway down his head. With the exception of John's father and his Killiecrankie mate, Tagger, no other locals had come in since they'd opened for business two nights earlier. If that trend continued, wages would have to come from somewhere other than profits, and that concerned her.

She was about to go out back and discuss the issue with Pete, when the door swung open and John came in. He sat down at the first table and pulled out a stubby from a paper bag.

'Working late tonight?' she asked him, in her role as a waitress.

'I had to drop a cat off at Trousers Point. It's difficult for me to get away from the place once I'm there.'

She decided against asking him why. 'How did it get a name like that?'

John avoided answering by looking around and asking a question of his own. 'Are you manning the stoves as well as the tables?'

'Just the tables. Pete's in the kitchen reading a book.'

'One with recipes in it, I hope.' He viewed the pine-board menu on the wall. 'Any chance of getting the same thing I had out at Patriarch Inlet?'

'This is a restaurant, not a fish and chip shop.'

He looked up at her with the hint of a smile. 'It was the best meal I've had this year.' He pulled a twenty-dollar bill out of his pocket. 'And I'm ready to spend up big to satisfy my selective tastes.'

She wondered if he'd been up at the hotel drinking with his father and Tagger. 'All right. Big money talks around here at the moment. As I wouldn't want Pete's cooking talents overly challenged, I'll send him out to keep you company, then start catering for your selective tastes myself.'

Saturday and Sunday nights John arrived at the same time with his usual stubby in a paper bag. He sat at the same table and ordered the same meal.

The Queensland couple was there again on Sunday night. Such was the effect the sparsely populated island had had on them that they greeted John as an acquaintance as soon as he arrived. After finishing off their bottle of wine, they wandered into the foyer and looked over some of the items on sale there. They took particular interest in Pete's sketches and asked John if he knew where they were drawn. He got up and told them, discussing each sketch as if it were his own.

After the couple left with four sketches under their arms, Jackson and John had the restaurant section to themselves. She finalised the takings, made cups of tea and sat down next to him for the first time in days. 'Sixty-six dollars from meals and two hundred and eighty-four dollars from sketches. Thanks, John. That just about matches our takings for the previous four nights.'

'Happy to help. Anyway, things should pick up when the tourist season hits full stride in a week or so.'

'It might be good if you were here when it does. The place could use a local art expert,' she said, tongue-in-cheek.

'Sorry. Vet work has first grab.'

'I thought you weren't due to go full-time for another four or five years yet.'

'Yeah, well…the idea of what constitutes part-time work is up for interpretation in the vet trade. But as my wombats are starting to get restless, tomorrow will be designated as a travel and vet supply delivery day. What're your plans?'

She eyed him with a questioning smile. 'I've got the next two days off, what' re my choices?'

'Anywhere south.'

'Trousers Point to start, then let's see what happens after that.'

Trousers Point – with its tree-studded headland and tumbled boulders, aqua sea and bone-white sand – wasn't quite what Jackson expected. Though when pressed by John to explain what she had expected, she could only shrug and mutter, 'It's beautiful.' Walking over the sand opened up her mind to shapes and colours again. She'd return and do some sketches of her own, she told him. Uni art work might as well start here, and The Sandman's might need such things.

'I just want to show you a spot nearby,' John said, after they'd returned and tied the wombats to the back of the flat tray again.

Two minutes later, they turned off the dirt road onto tyre tracks, went through a gap in a row of tall blue gums and drove on over the undulating paddock to where grass met heath and rocks. They stopped and looked out over the sand and ocean again.

'Of all the top spots on the island, this is where I most want to live,' he said, watching her.

'It's fantastic. I'd want to live here too,' she answered brightly, caught up in the moment.

The next day, while the wombats occupied the flat-tray, they climbed Mt Strzelecki. On the windswept summit, they watched the island brighten and dim under shifting sunlight and cloud shadow.

John pointed out Whitemark and Lady Barron and named the nearby islands, before narrowing his eyes and looking south to a distant coastline. Again, he pointed. 'Our mainland, north-east Tassie,' he said, as if it were the first time he'd ever seen it. 'You can just make it out.'

Feeling on top of the world up there, she rested her head on his shoulder and told him she was coming back here as well, with a sketchbook and pencils. He could come too if he wanted.

The following morning, with a double canoe strapped on top of the flat-tray and the wombats left on the farm, they drove to a property east of Lady Barron. A squinting, white-haired old couple – Mary and Arthur – greeted them on the veranda of their low stone house.

John just managed to introduce Jackson before Mary blurted

out, 'Well, we're pleased you two got out here to see us, isn't that so, Arthur?'

Once Arthur confirmed that with a nod, they were shooed towards cushioned chairs and told to sit down. Mary went inside and Arthur drew up another chair and eased himself into it as if it were about to break. An old border collie laboured up and plopped down beside him.

Eyeing his dog, Arthur said, 'I've had a tough time keeping those back legs of his movin' this past winter.'

'How old is he now?' John asked, knowing the answer. Rubbing his knees with gnarled hands, Arthur named the exact date the dog was born. 'So he'll be fifteen in three weeks' time.'

'Getting on a bit, isn't he?'

'No more than most.'

'Let's have a look at you then, Jake.' John inspected the dog's teeth, moved his hands along its body and legs, as he'd seen Sam do so many times before. 'Other than some arthritis, weight for age he's as fit as any dog I've seen in a long time.'

That's what Arthur wanted to hear. His eyes brightened and his mouth lifted into a gap-toothed smile.

John took out a packet of tablets and handed them to him. 'More cortisone from Sam. When the nights go cold, feed him one of these nightly. It'll make a difference.'

'I will. You know, John, we keep him inside with us at night, so it won't be hard to do.'

'Going on about Jake again, are you?' Mary said, shuffling out the door with a silver tray stacked in cups and saucers, a pot of tea and cakes. 'As if the island hasn't heard enough about the workings of that poor old dog.' She placed the tray on a table. 'Well, come on then, you two, get your tongues around this.' She poured tea and passed around cakes, then sat down as tentatively as her husband had. 'Are you from around here, my dear?' she asked Jackson next to her. Mary knew she wasn't.

After Jackson told her where home was and why she was here, Mary said, 'We've talked about going to Melbourne one day and having a good look around, haven't we, Arthur?' She paused for Arthur's confirming nod. 'But we haven't got there yet. Still, we don't suffer here, do we, Arthur?'

Patting Jackson on the knee, she went on, 'You know, love, we've got air so pure people are bottling it and selling it to the mainlanders. Isn't that so, Arthur? The ocean's so clear you can duck under at the beach end and see whales migrating the Pacific. Can't you, Arthur? We've got soil so rich…'

Two hours later, following more tea and cakes, lunch and a tour of the property, John and Jackson managed to finally break away and get back in the flat-tray. They drove down the track to Cameron's Inlet, glazed in ducks and sunshine. But with other vet deliveries to make, and The Sandman's due to open in a few hours, there was only time to look around.

Arthur and Mary stood up slowly and waved together as they passed by the house again, heading out. Jackson waved back, smiling. She'd never spent so much time with such old people before.

*

A cold easterly blew in off the ocean.

Gutbuster pulled his red beanie down over his ears, switched on his torch and checked the time: nine o'clock. He grabbed his petrol can and wound his way out of the trees down to the shack. Through the unlocked door he went, torchlight piercing the darkness. He went straight for the wood stove. Locating a fire iron, he yanked the stove open and prodded away at a burning log until it flipped out on the floor. He poured petrol in a circle around the log, then bolted for the door spilling more petrol as he went.

Back up in the trees again, he barely had time to turn around before flames shot up and swelled.

Windows burst. Sparks flew.

Fire leapt out snapping with heat.

Photo time! From Nick's daypack, Gutbuster took out his other present from Harris – Nick's Nikon Coolpix 995 digital camera. It seemed fitting that the camera should be used where Nick had performed his last act as a Dragon, before being retired. So that's what Gutbuster did.

A minute later he started sweating in the heat. He moved further away, sat down against a second tree trunk, took off his beanie and watched the shack burn to the ground.

Job satisfaction didn't get any better than this.

*

Standing on the bridge of Harris's Haines Hunter 620SC, Big Butch looked at his watch: nine-fifteen. On the low headland a fiery glow – like a bright orange fist – rose from where once an old hermit's lonely shack had stood. Big Butch grabbed his binoculars and watched as the glow stretched to flames that danced into the clear black night.

Half an hour later, over the idling of the twin Evinrude Oceanpro 225 outboards, Big Butch picked up the sound of the distant runabout returning. He turned on the running lights and checked the boarding ladder on the boat's stern.

Then a plan began to form in Big Butch's mind. The closest he'd ever come to this sort of luxury was in browsing through magazines in the BMW and yacht owners-only section of the local newsagency. And the five hours he'd spent doing the captain's course, then getting up here, had swelled his imagination with other big-money possibilities: sea-view mansions, marinas and maxis, imported cigars, grass and grog, a full-size Pot Black snooker table. When this job was over, he wanted to be around this sort of luxury again, permanently. So, how could he make that happen? Start with what's nearest and dearest, he thought. This ocean-going palace had to be worth at least a couple of million dollars. And word had it on the back streets that Harris – as someone else – had recently bought another one and berthed it up on the Gold Coast. Big Butch had always wanted to go to the Gold Coast.

He looked around quickly to ensure that Harris hadn't suddenly come aboard attached to a parachute or a scuba tank. Satisfied he was still alone, Big Butch let his mind wander again. He had the keys to the boat, its dry-dock tractor and storage garage. And judging from the dirt and droppings, the cobwebs and insect life he and Gutbuster had cleaned off

125

the boat prior to coming up here, it was obvious that boating didn't hold a high priority in Harris's life at the moment. So what if he got more keys cut, got the registration papers reworked, gave the boat a re-spray and sold it quickly through the back street classifieds for about half its worth? Then he'd only have to concern himself with a one-way ride up the coast in his new BMW before settling into a big Gold Coast hotel and studying the tropical classifieds for his marina-attached dream home.

He'd have to take a lesson from dead Nick's book, though. The ticket to paradise came only after Harris went the way of Nick and those other promotion-minded team members he'd dispatched.

So, fork-in-the-road time – which way to go? Right, left, straight? Rich, dead or continue to work for small-room money? Water splashing off the runabout's hull signalled he had about a minute to make his decision, while his thumping heart reminded him that such decisions weren't meant to be easy. Finally, he decided.

He repositioned the ladder on the hidden, seaward side of the bow, then unscrewed the ladder joints in two places until they were on their last thread. Gutbuster was loyalty-bound to Harris and committed to living in lifelong poverty. He was also a non-swimmer and a quick sinker with a little help. Returning solo meant Big Butch would have to stow the boat fast, without fanfare, then ring up and report before going bush and planning how he'd take Harris out. He'd only get one try at it, so it had to be right. After so many years of dependable service, though, at least he'd have surprise on his side.

23

Pete's tired eyes turned away from the charred litter and drifting smoke. 'They were my only photos, Santi,' he mumbled, before wandering down to the shoreline and continuing.

Constable Mitchell in a four-wheel drive, Jackson and John in one flat-tray and Rex and Tagger in another one, drove up. Jackson spotted Pete first and raced off after him. When she caught up, neither of them spoke. Squelching sand and an early sea breeze were all that disturbed the silence before they sat down and stared out to sea.

A few minutes later, the constable approached with a red beanie in his hand. He showed it to Pete. 'Yours?' he asked.

'No.'

Jackson thought she recognised it. 'There was a big hulk of a man in at The Sandman's Friday night who was wearing it, or one exactly like it.' She kept her eyes on the constable's. 'This was no accident, was it?'

'I suspect not.' He surveyed the ocean as if the culprit might still be out there somewhere. 'Give some thought to that red beanie man, okay?' he said to Jackson, his eyes fixed on the horizon. 'I'd like to get a description of him before you leave.' He turned and went back to the smouldering remains.

'If I hadn't come here in October, none of this would have happened,' Jackson said.

'You could say the same thing about me coming here when I did.' He turned to her, his eyes wet, but with a resigned look on his face. 'So what are you like with a hammer and nails?'

Islanders who'd never met Pete came throughout the day. They walked around the wreckage and nodded their greetings to Pete's friends sitting on the rocks. After surveying the embers and ash without comment, and absorbing the view, they returned to their vehicles and drove off.

That night no jokes were told at the Whitemark Hotel. Cribbage, darts and eight-ball didn't feature in the night's activities. Beer flowed, however, as the crowd in the front bar discussed the rebuilding of an uninsured shack most had never known existed and could not understand why it had been torched. But torched it had been, and that angered people, and questions about why it happened weren't going to get the shack back up.

Flanked by locals and Pete and Jackson, Russell – a former boat builder down from Northeast River for the night – drew up a set of plans. Completed, the plans were fast-tracked and given council approval by a show of hands.

Talk turned to those who could afford time the following day to help with the clean-up. It seemed most everyone could.

An eight-ball roster was summoned. Requests were made and the roster filled in with donors of building materials stored away in warehouses and backyard sheds.

When a retired mate of Russell's made known his wish to re-enter the carpentry trade, a second roster was summoned, and the following headings pencilled in: FOUNDATIONS AND POUR CONCRETE / FLOORS AND WALLS / ROOFING / ELECTRICALS / PLUMBING / PAINTING AND FINISHING OFF.

Initially, names were to go in one column only. The problem was everyone wanted to hone up on their different building skills at the same time. So Tagger placed his Geelong cap upside-down on the bar. Names on paper were tossed in and drawn back out, and labourers assigned their three-day stints, with their names recorded on the roster.

Rosters filled, Louise poured fresh drinks and announced they were 'compliments of the house'.

Tongues loosened, and for the first time people had to raise their voices to be heard. That arson had, up to now, been a mainland word was noted. That mainland problems were drawing closer, threatening the reasons why people chose to live here, followed that.

Constable Mitchell came in. Spotting Tagger and Rex, he went over and drew them aside. 'No suspicious types came in by plane,' he said.

'By boat up the coast then,' Tagger, a former senior constable, responded. 'After the clean-up, I'll fly over to Launceston, borrow a car and nose around the north-east coast. I've a couple of mates who're still breathing there. They might be good for some information.'

That the problem might be quarantined if the arsonist was nabbed prompted more talk.

'I'll ask around down south,' a Lady Barron fisherman piped up. 'Someone may have spotted something unusual.'

'I'll do the same up north,' the former boat builder responded.

Louise called for 'last drinks' earlier than usual. Nobody bothered to ask her why.

*

While the islanders continued to measure up, saw and hammer away at the shack site, an appreciative Pete told Rex one day that he could pay for the rebuilding.

But Rex barely listened. 'When the mood's like this,' he said, 'it goes beyond money. There's a feelin' around that everyone's been burned by the arsonist. And that the only way to hit back is to come together, get things rebuilt fast, then find a vantage point – like up the top of Strzelecki – and shout, "It's back up, you bastard! Try it again and we'll use your guts for bricking mortar."' He smiled. 'You can't beat exercises like this for fosterin' community spirit, now can you? Once the shack's back up, photos of it'll be taken, enlarged and hung up behind the hotel bar. Islanders'll be crowin' about it for generations. By closin' time each night, the topic'll be bigger than Grand Final Day. Parliament House in Canberra will be a dog kennel compared to The Sandman's Patriarch Inlet Wilderness Lodge.'

'Then I'll just have to think of other ways to repay people here,' Pete said, enjoying Rex's company more than ever.

It took three weeks for the shack to be completely rebuilt. The night after it was finished, Tagger came into the front bar sporting a self-satisfied look. 'The wheels are moving, gentlemen, the wheels are moving,' he repeated to the bevy of mystified faces when asked for news. 'I should know more in the next couple of days.'

After getting a beer, he took Pete aside. 'For your ears and the good constable's alone, I can confirm a sighting. A big, distinctly foreign, moon-struck boat was seen by fishermen off Clarke Island beating a fast tune south not long after the arson attack. Additionally, a mate and I have been doing some detective work. The short story is, fishermen's witness statements and a detailed description of a big Haines Hunter motor launch – currently residing in a locked double garage at Musselroe Bay – have been provided to both the Tasmanian and Victorian Police Departments. As well, if Victorian police don't get in touch with me in the next forty-eight hours, they know I'll be contacting the press.'

He gulped his beer down, then gave Pete a wink and a grin. 'Your shout, I believe.'

By the time Louise called 'Stumps' at 3 a.m., an island holiday had been declared to nurse approaching hangovers and the rebuilding program had achieved an exalted status not rivalled since the hotel's first foundation stone was laid over a century earlier.

Before going, Pete quickly double checked with Rex the list of labourers' names he'd collected. That done, he added the heading 'The Sandman's Free Meal Winners', and pinned the list on the Eight-ball and Darts Club noticeboard.

24

So busy were they at The Sandman's that John volunteered to wait on tables for a couple of hours a night while Jackson helped Pete in the kitchen.

Free meal winners – half the island's population in John's estimation – occupied all six tables minutes after the place opened. Bookings had to be made and closing time extended. With money still filling their pockets, locals then went up to the pub to spend it. Rex and Tagger reckoned that the hotel had experienced a business boom since free meals started being redeemed at The Sandman's. What the hotel didn't sell in meals, they were well and truly making up for in drinks.

Island touring continued over the next couple of weeks. After more tea and cakes at Mary's and Arthur's, canoeing and sketching featured at Cameron's Inlet. Jackson surprised John there by kissing him quickly and playfully and seconds later thought how long it had taken for that to happen. After that, hands reached for hands and arms encircled waists and shoulders as if they'd been re-programmed to do that before doing anything else.

Up the north-west coast they went. At Long Point they swam, cooked sausages, kissed and began exploring each other more. They took in an Aboriginal history lesson at Wyabelena, and were taken out to Prime Seal Island for fishing.

At Killiecrankie, Tagger met them at the shop. After pointing out 'the only grounded telephone box north of Whitemark', he escorted them along the beach and up a steep headland to look for legendary diamonds amongst the huge granite boulders.

Three days later, at power pole 154 just north of Killiecrankie, they turned onto a disused track and wound past ragged gum trees towards the coast.

'Dad found this track a long time ago,' John mentioned as they bounced over rocks and skirted potholes big enough to fall into. 'He used to bring Mum here in the early days. Few locals even know about it.'

It was the roughest ride Jackson had ever experienced, but at the end of it was the reward – a sandy cove secluded by granite boulders the size of small houses, and an aqua sea laced in shallow reefs and protruding rocks. There was no indication anyone had ever been here. Even the seagulls were missing.

When John turned off the engine, the stillness was palpable, like the world had suddenly stopped.

'It's worth a look, don't you think?'

Jackson kissed him softly, cheek to ear to turning mouth. 'It's worth more than that,' she said, grabbing her bag and sliding out the door. 'I'm going to change. You can too if you want.'

A minute later, Jackson strode down to the water in her now familiar red bikini and took small, torturous steps wading in. She raised her arms as if they were allergic to the sea, and glanced around. 'Well, come on down!' she shouted to him like a quiz show host, then she laughed, delighted with everything.

He took off his T-shirt, shoes and socks, then paused to watch her plunge into the water and swim frantically around before hopping up and hugging herself.

'I'll have to find other company if you don't get in here with me!' she shouted again.

John exchanged his jeans for bathers, grabbed the beach tent and blanket and got out. It took him a few minutes to erect the tent in the sand and carpet it in blanket. Then he moved to the waterline and dived in after her. When he stood up again and put his arms around her, she moved against him, put her mouth to his ear and played the initiator's role again.

'If you want to make love, John,' and there was no doubting that he did, 'it's safe to, and I can't think of a better place than here, or a better time than now.'

Her feet didn't touch the ground again until they were well inside the tent.

Afterwards, as they lay there in the tent looking out at the sea, John asked, 'Do you think you'd like to do a sketch of this place sometime as well?'

She snuggled closer, stroking his face and kissing him. 'Uh huh.'

'If the sketch includes us, I'd like to be around when you do it, just in case your memory wants refreshing.'

'What about tomorrow?'

*

The office phone rang just as Constable Mitchell was about to lock up for the night and head home. Emitting a frustrated growl, he returned to his desk and answered it. 'Constable Mitchell.'

'Constable, this is Assistant Superintendent Jim Roberts, St Kilda CIB. I won't keep you long. I'm just ringing to personally thank you for the valuable information you provided us regarding the arson attack down there a few weeks ago. In response to that information and other crucial information that's come our way the past fortnight, former Detective Inspector Michael Harris was arrested this morning at his Brighton home. He's been charged with numerous arson-related offences, as well as trafficking in illegal drugs. Harris's passport has been confiscated. Bail has been set at one hundred and fifty thousand dollars and committal proceedings are currently under way. We have yet to locate his other two accomplices. Hopefully we'll get them in the next few days. I'd like to thank you again, constable. In the coming weeks I'll ensure that you're kept up-to-date with further developments.'

*

The first person to come into The Sandman's that night was Ben.

The second, a moment later, was Constable Mitchell, who went straight for the kitchen door. 'Pete in the back?' he asked Jackson, not bothering to stop.

'Yes.'

With Mitchell gone, there was just Ben again with a slightly bemused look on his face. As he closed the distance between them, Jackson noticed his scar had faded and he'd put on weight.

'The lady at the hotel told me you were here. How're things?'

Awesome, until now, she thought. She glared up at him. 'I don't believe this. Why are you here?'

'I hope to know the answer to that in the next few minutes.'

'Wrong, Ben. Try again. Why are you here?'

'I'm just a pilgrim for your love,' he sang roughly.

'You're hardly Eric Clapton.'

'Musically, no. But we've shared similar experiences. Like sampling the underside of life and coming out of it clean, ready to do things differently.'

'Well, I'm pleased for the both of you.' And she was, at least for Ben.

'So anyway, I thought…you know, we might initially talk and…'

Rex and Tagger banged the screen door noisily, before coming in and sitting down at the first table. Tagger took out a bottle of wine.

'I'm working now, Ben, and it's going to get very busy.'

'No hurry. I haven't eaten since breakfast.' He went and sat down at a back table.

Jackson took glasses over to Rex and Tagger and opened their bottle. Doing that steadied her nerves. 'Is there a beer strike on?' she asked.

'I wish there had been last night,' Rex answered.

'If you're proposing one for the future, we'll support it,' Tagger said, pouring the wine. 'Anyway, we've brought along the cure. Pete cooking tonight?'

'Of course. Who else would be?'

'It's just that John mentioned you've been cookin' up his favourite fish dish for him whenever he's been in.'

She thought fast. 'Just to give him the chance to talk to Pete about plants and hothouses. You know the sort of thing.'

A group of tourists entered and sat down at the next table.

'Right. Well, the rush has started. We'd best order,' Tagger warned, 'or we'll be late getting up the road to share Groper's birthday drink.'

'Didn't we do that last night?'

'Oh.' Tagger put on the same stunned look Jackson had minutes earlier. 'Not sure.' He gave a grin the devil would be proud of. 'Best we do it again just to be on the safe side.'

Pausing on the way to the kitchen, Jackson asked Ben what he wanted to eat.

'That favourite fish dish sounds all right.'

'Fish and chips then. Listen, Ben, we can't talk now. Where are you staying tonight?'

'I thought you might have the answer to that one.' There was no faulting the consistency of his replies.

'Bed and breakfast at the hotel costs fifty dollars a night.' She was intent on looking him straight in the eye, her gaze defiant – though feelings for him still flickered away. 'We close at ten. If you want to come back, we can talk then.'

More locals came in, followed by John.

'John boy. Sit down here with us,' Tagger called out.

'I can't. I still have one more stop to make.' He glanced from Jackson to Ben, before his eyes settled on Jackson again. 'A late delivery up at Wyabelena. It includes a meal. So can we meet up at the hotel after you're finished here?' he asked.

'Okay.' Ben's presence made it impossible for Jackson to say anything more.

'See you then.' John left quickly.

'So it's the three of us for the hotel, is it?' Ben asked her quietly.

'Yes. Two downstairs and one upstairs.' Jackson turned on her heel and went into the kitchen.

*

'West coast of Tasmania,' Ben replied. 'With its mountains, thick bush and constant rain, it's like a ghost land, invisible to the rest of the world. Which in my situation was perfect. So I got healthy and got a job working on some back roads. They're supposing people in big cars will want to use them someday.'

The screen door eased shut as the last customers left.

'You feel I can be trusted knowing all this now?' Jackson asked.

'You always could. It was just the spooks who might've been hovering around you who couldn't be.'

'Had a paranoia check lately, Ben?'

Trophy smile time returned. 'No need to now. The important thing is it's safe to re-enter the world back in Melbourne again.' He reached for her hand, which she allowed him to hold while vowing that things wouldn't go any further than this. 'And I was hoping that us getting back together would follow.'

'I start uni in a week.'

'Good. I'm making a new start too – part-time study, part time work of the legal sort – with just the occasional lash at the surf.' He'd had a lot of experience probing her eyes, as well as her emotions and conscience, as he did now.

She drew her hand away. 'I've got a boyfriend here.'

'Yeah, I know. Farm boy. It happens. But he'll be here and we'll be back in the real world.'

25

Though John had left the tent up at the cove, the next morning they headed south and that surprised Jackson. She said nothing, though, concentrating instead on the paddocks, the sea, Ben, and the arrest of that bent copper Pete had told her about. What troubled her was that 'arson-related offences and trafficking in illegal drugs' were not all Harris had been involved in.

'What about intentionally naming over people and killing them?' she'd blurted out to Pete in the kitchen.

'I wouldn't be surprised if other more serious offences are still being investigated. Anyway, Constable Mitchell is being kept informed.'

Jackson thought about how the Victorian Police could be informed about those 'other more serious offences' without her having to do the informing. Ben was the other witness. With some coaxing, would he be willing to go to the police? Jackson doubted it. His book on the past was locked, its key thrown away.

At Trousers Point they drove through the line of blue gums again to the paddock that overlooked the coastline. They got out and walked along rocks until they found one flat enough to sit on together.

John spoke first. 'That bloke in at the restaurant last night, was he a friend of yours?'

He'd always been open and honest with her, so she'd be the same with him…well, up to a point. 'His name's Ben. He was here a couple of months ago, and until then he was my boyfriend.'

'Ah, one of the blokes who was asking around for you. So why is here now?'

She rested her head against his arm and looked out to sea. 'He wants us to get back together after I get back home next week.'

John was slow to answer. 'As he's come back here, that must be very important for him. Do you think it'll happen?'

'No.'

The sea held them a while, before John said, 'Do you remember when I told you that if I could live anywhere on the island it would be here? And you said you felt the same.'

Any lingering thoughts of Harris and Ben disappeared. The caution flag went up. 'If I intended living on the island permanently, I meant.'

'Yeah, I know that. After I become a vet, I will be living here permanently, right on this very spot. Dad bought the land for me after Mum left. We spent weeks planting those blue gums back there, and the farmer across the road's been running sheep here ever since to keep the grass down.'

'Right. Well, you're very lucky. It's beautiful.'

'Yeah.' He jumped topics. 'Pete told me he'd asked you to come back over the Easter holidays to work for him.'

'He did, yes. He's talking about closing the place next week and reopening it then.' Missing John's touch, she put her arm round his waist. 'I'm just not sure what things are going to be like in Melbourne. So I said I'd let him know closer to the time.'

For a full minute his eyes didn't budge from the sea. Then he dropped his head and said, 'I know I'm going to lose you if you don't come back at Easter.'

Not knowing what to say, she pretended she did. 'John, making love with someone isn't a mandatory prescription for signing a long-term relationship contract.' What a mouthful that was. Had she read it somewhere? It felt as though she were reciting someone else's words. As an idea it sounded cool, so in control and worldly to her. The problem was, those characteristics described others, not her.

'Listen, I'll say this once, then I promise I won't burden you with anything like it again, unless you're here at Easter.' He kept his eyes on the sea. 'You are what I dream about. Yes, having this land's great, but my biggest stroke of luck has been being with you. And I just don't want to think about that not happening in the future.' He shrugged, perhaps as a sign that he'd bared his heart: it was in her hands now, so there was no more to be said on the topic.

A minute later he got up. 'Want to go for that walk now?' he asked.

*

John didn't come into the restaurant that night.

Ben did, just before closing time, with a sombre look on his face. He sat down at the same table. 'I missed you today,' he said, as she waited for his order. 'It's senseless, isn't it, me sticking around here?' When he didn't get an answer, he blew out his cheeks and sighed. 'What's obvious to me is that I'm going to need a hometown advantage to get back in step with you. So I'm flying out in the morning. New starts begin when you get back.'

She nodded in acknowledgement, though he interpreted the nod as agreement. 'Just confidentially, Ben, did you know that the copper who ran that addict down in the car park has been arrested?'

'Really?' The topic had obviously been deleted from his big interest list. His eyes dropped to his shifting feet, John-like. 'A good thing, I suppose. But it's got nothing to do with us any more.'

She waited for something upbeat, like 'What happened is just a blink in the past, Jack. Our aim is straight for the future now.' But it didn't come. His confidence must be down, she thought.

After Ben left, Jackson went out to the kitchen and interrupted Pete's dishwashing. Talk was foremost on her mind, and he was the only person on the island she wanted to talk to now. When they were seated out front, she started, 'Ben's got this idea in his head that we'll be getting back together after I leave here.'

'Did he tell you that he came in this afternoon and apologised for taking my car? I admired that. It took courage.'

Why couldn't Pete just have said something simple like 'Oh'? Typical of him: always dwelling on the positive side of things, always balancing things up. But she wasn't prepared to concede the point. 'It's all a part of his get healthy, fix up the romantic past and make a new start campaign.'

'New starts are important.'

On that, Pete was an authority. 'I know they are, but his happen about every six months.' Her mind flashed back to that first-week swap meet: her rubbish roller blades traded for a prize bike, the bike for a gold watch and so on and so on. 'There's something in him that's never satisfied, that always thinks there's got to be more to everything in life.'

'A natural explorer. People like that can be fun and exciting to be around.'

'Or dangerous.'

'Part of the excitement, I guess.' Pete pushed the conversation along. 'They're interesting contrasts, aren't they, John and Ben? One happily island-bound, having had his one-track future worked out since the day he picked up his first wombat. The other big-city street-smart, working the fringe areas, living on a knife edge.' He made a point of pausing and smiling at her. 'But with a genuinely likeable nature… And you involved with both, feeling what you do for them.'

Pete got up and went over to the drink-making machine. '"Nothing better than a cup of tea at times like these," Santi always says. "It adds perspective to the discussion of difficult topics." She gets that wordy at times.'

After handing Jackson her drink, he sat back down. 'There's one point to all this you've avoided talking about, and after you decide that, all else will follow.'

She looked at him fondly for a moment before going on, 'do you know John has property at Trousers Point?'

'Rex has mentioned it.'

'And that he eventually wants to get a bank loan and build a house on it?'

'It won't be much of a loan. You know what people are like here. Donate or discount your building materials, and toss in the labour for free, especially for him. The chance to get some credits up with the future vet will draw people in from all corners.'

'I know him so well now. If I come back here over Easter, he'll want me to go the next step.'

'Which is?' He wanted her to say it.

'Be with him all my non-working hours.' She could have said more, but only to John.

'A normal wish for someone who feels what he does for you.' She used her up-turned hands for emphasis. 'But don't you see, Pete? It's terrible leaving him now, so what would it be like if we got even closer?'

'Difficult.' He sipped his tea, then stared at his mug for a moment. 'You know, there's an old saying about someone who becomes the fabric of another person's life. Obviously, you've become that in John's.'

'But all that could so easily change.'

'Not with John. You know that... I guess the question is how much John's become the fabric of your life?'

'I'm only eighteen, Pete.'

'Just starting out, I know.'

She recalled the day Nick said that. 'There are other reasons for not making Easter commitments, Pete. There'll be new responsibilities, new people and things I'll have to do back in Melbourne.'

He folded his arms over his chest. 'All that happens, yes.'

'And I'll have to find part-time work. Employers aren't into employees making up their own work rosters.'

'They are here. And I'll double whatever holiday wages they're prepared to offer you.'

She laughed for the first time since being up at the cove. 'With free meals thrown in to keep the unions off your back.'

'Three-course ones.'

Then the front door opened and John came in. After Pete slipped out back, Jackson stood up and greeted him. There was beer on his breath, but no other indication that he'd tried to keep up with his father and Tagger.

'Do you want to come up to the hotel, or go for a drive or anything?' he asked, hope blooming.

'Not now, John. But tomorrow we're closed. I'll meet you here and it'll be your choice where we go.'

*

Again he surprised her. As their holiday time together shrank, so too did the distances covered touring the island, Jackson thought, while they took a short walk out to the end of the jetty.

Sitting down on the worn bench, John opened up the roll of chart paper he'd brought and draped it over their laps. 'This is a rough plan for the house at Trousers Point,' he said, without looking at her. 'Russell drew it up at the hotel last night.'

While John pointed out the features of the double-storey house, Jackson wondered if she'd lost some years in her life: surely she was still eighteen, not thirty. For the moment, though, it was useless to remind him of that with an assembly line of housing terms coming her way thick and fast. Corrugated iron and brick exterior. Dome-shaped roof with solar heating panels. Glazed windows. Open-plan living downstairs with a lounge room, built-in kitchen, dining area, a bedroom, big wood heater, toilet and a bathroom with a spa bath. Upstairs were two more bedrooms with built-in closets and big window views. Outside, a double garage and shed, paving-stone driveway, barbecue and garden area, a cubby house and swing set…

At that point she could no longer hold her tongue. 'What?'

He stopped and looked around sheepishly. 'Over time, not right away. Anyway, what do you think?' he asked.

'Terrific.' She doubted she'd ever said that word faster. Why couldn't he just stick to beach tents?

After a sea-scanning pause, John asked, 'Can you think of anything else that should go on the plans?'

A helicopter ramp for a quick escape skipped through her mind. 'No.'

It was like the sea held magnets to their faces again.

'My plane leaves at ten in the morning,' she said finally. 'I can get transport out to the airport tomorrow.'

'No, don't do that. I want to take you.'

Jackson got up first, and they walked around Whitemark saying little. An hour later, back outside The Sandman's, she turned to him. 'So nine-thirty tomorrow, okay?' She didn't want to go through the ordeal of seeing him again that night.

He nodded and left.

Her plane was on the tarmac with its engines running the next day when they arrived. After checking in her bags, she kissed him quickly, not game to look him in the eyes. 'Bye.'

'Bye.'

She turned and rushed out the departure door.

*

Harris put The Eagles' *Hell Freezes Over* in the DVD player, turned up the volume and went over and popped a bottle of imported champagne. After sampling a glass of it and reaching for a slice of imported salmon, he strolled out onto the vast deck of his Brighton cliff-top home and gazed down at the smaller roofs, swimming pools and manicured trees and gardens littering the landscape below.

As always, his skin tingled with pride and satisfaction at just how high he'd come over the years. True, he didn't make police commissioner. And with the current rash of gangland hits and paybacks tarnishing local street life, business had taken a noticeable downturn. So the price of his bail was looking a bit more than just pocket change at the moment. Still, after hiring a top defence lawyer, sprinkling some cash around and terminating Big Butch and Gutbuster – the prosecutor's only potential plea-bargaining witnesses now – it wouldn't be long before the Harris Express was back on the business rails again, steaming ahead at full throttle.

After a second glass of champagne, he'd head down to a phone booth to ring up Qantas, then Big Butch and Gutbuster, currently holed-up in the Tasmanian bush. Once he'd provided them with their flight details, he'd invite them to the Criterion Hotel for a de-briefing reunion and counter tea – his shout. The convenience of a back-door entry from the now brightly lit car park would be emphasised. Then, following car park target practice – 'pop pop, pop pop' – with his silencer-attached revolver, he'd celebrate the abrupt end of the prosecution's case against him by eating at the trendiest café south of Toorak – The Brighton Cliffs Inn – just three minutes' drive from home.

Harris's thoughts were diverted by a lower-level, sweetly tight-arsed member of the lycra gear and outdoor café set. She was leashed to an immaculately coiffured poodle and jogging in slow time down the scenic walking track towards that very same Brighton Cliffs Inn. He reached for his telescope and looked down over the railing, focusing in on places groin-stirring when someone suddenly commented in his ear, 'Good view, huh? Maybe you should get a bit closer.'

Spinning round, he was hit by a shattering hip and shoulder to the ribcage that sent him tumbling over the railing. It was Big Butch up there shouting, 'Downsizing, Harris! The, oh balls, whatever!' But only for three very long seconds.

26

David and his MX5, top down, were at Moorabin to pick her up. 'I'm mother-sent and carrying her apologies,' he said, teeth flashing. 'She's running a bit late at home.' After strapping her bags to the boot rack, David offered her sunglasses, gloves, a neck scarf and a bucket-shaped fur hat to match his own for the ride back into the city. 'Mother-tested and approved,' he continued, chuckling to himself.

She didn't have the heart to say no and watch his face deflate.

Clothing additions in place, he shoved John Butler Trio's *Sunrise Over The Sea* into the CD player, gunned the engine, and they were off, out of the car park and on to the Tullamarine Freeway, zipping past traffic with their scarves flapping and the trio's 'Zebra' reverberating in their wake.

'Oh, there you are, Jackson,' her mother said, as they came through the door. Turning from the mirror, her mother embraced her loosely – so as not to disturb her make-up and hair – and kissed the air noisily. 'David and I are grabbing a bite to eat, then catching a show at The Regent. There's a casserole in the fridge. Oh, and that Ben fellow's been ringing up. He wants you to ring him back.' She glanced down at her cleavage, adjusted it quickly then fastened her eyes on David standing there in the open doorway. 'I could have used more time.' A little tentatively, she extended her arms out to him for an assessment. 'How's this?' She looked suddenly vulnerable.

'Beeeeeautiful!'

She brightened quickly and took control again. 'We'll have to preserve me then. Mazda top up?'

'Already done.'

Margaret turned and eyed her daughter for a moment, before taking her hand. The one-mother whirlwind act slowed. 'I want you to know,' she said, 'that I've really, really missed you.' Before Jackson could say anything, her mother swung around and appealed to David. 'What about this? Two leisurely courses at the restaurant then back here for a daughter de-briefing and French pastry for dessert? We can do The Regent tomorrow night, don't you think, David?'

'Easily.'

Her eyes held on to his for a moment. 'How did I ever get to be this lucky?'

As rewards, both David and Jackson got light pecks on the cheek, despite Margaret's lipstick splash. Then Jackson watched them leave, trying to get used to all this again.

In the kitchen, she put the casserole in the microwave and thought about ringing Ben. The point was, by doing that she'd be responding to him here as she had in the past. And things were different now, despite what he thought would happen in the future. Yet, did that mean burying the feelings she still had for him and ignoring him? As she was considering this, the phone rang. Not surprisingly, it was Ben, with his opening line only slightly changed.

'Good to hear your voice so close again, Jack.'

What had happened to 'Satin voice'? She needed to choose her words carefully, so she started with the basics. 'How are you?'

'With you back, terrific. Listen, I've got my most important things-to-do list here in front of me right now,' the man of lists noted, 'and this is how it reads so far. Living back in the backyard mansion, tick. Enrol in a business course, tick. Twenty hours' work a week at Patrick Warehouse, tick. Reclaim my car, tick. The next item, which is at the very top of the list, reads "New start – tonight with Jack", and I've got my biro poised.'

'I can't, Ben. I'm tired and I need to unpack.' She wasn't and she didn't, but no way was she going to take on the role of instant, be-there-when-you-want-me girlfriend again.

'Then I'll just change tonight to tomorrow.'

'Monash, and I'll be looking for my own twenty hours of work a week.' That *was* true.

'Then I'll just change tomorrow to tomorrow night.'

Being with him had to occur sometime, didn't it? 'All right… We'll be staying well clear of the Criterion Hotel, though, won't we?' Was she joking? Not entirely, she decided. After all, that night had been their last night out together.

He chuckled. 'The place doesn't exist. Strapped In are playing at the Shark's Tooth. Pick you up at ten.'

*

The strobe-lit Shark's Tooth was packed when they arrived. That's the way Ben always liked his clubs. Empty space was for bird life, not people. The more people there were to crunch, the more American grip handshakes, high-five and touched knuckle greetings there were to perform, drinks to share, girls to kiss and wrap his arms around, the happier he was.

Tonight too, this rejuvenated master of charm quickly spotted people he knew. He led Jackson over to them, taking a mystery water bottle out of his back pocket. In answer to the question about his recent whereabouts, words again slid effortlessly off his tongue. 'At the Snowy Mountain Fasting and Meditation Convention. Heard of it? Spirited right away, I was. So it took a while to abseil down and ply the bush tracks to get back here.' He raised his bottle for all to see, then took a performance swig and swooned. 'Pure Snowy Mountain spring water. Fantastic! And the good news is I've got more out in the limo, going for one celebratory night only, at the lowest of all discount prices – nothing. So line up, water winners, and place your order. Ben the benevolent is back in town.'

The contorted face next to her responded, 'Ah get rid of it ya wanker and I'll get ya a beer.'

Jackson had to smile. Never knowing what to expect, she was reminded that – yes – being with Ben was fun, usually. And yes, apologising to Pete for taking his car was commendable of him, though it was convenient too.

In one group after another, his script stayed the same. By the time he'd finished his fifth free beer, Benevolent Ben – the nightclub philosopher and spring water devotee version – had well and truly settled in again. He lifted his arms to the gods of strobe light and rejoiced. 'The nightmare's over, Jack, never to be repeated! We're back! We can feel it in our dust-filled bones! The high-voltage current of big city life and our life pump – clubbing time!'

She thought he might leap onto the dance floor as John Travolta from *Staying Alive*, mother Margaret's favourite DVD. He didn't, not immediately, anyway. Instead, he unveiled his wallet and ran a gauntlet of grinning faces to the bar. As she watched the gulf between them widen, it seemed to her that Ben's latest new start was really just a continuation, less his near-death detour through the underside of life. She believed him when he said it was an experience never to be repeated. He wasn't into repetition. She was pleased she'd come and witnessed him working this place and his friends again. He'd recovered – fully. Though he might claim differently, he didn't need her now. Her replacements were all around them with their glazed eyes and flushed faces, flicking their hair and giggling loudly at his jokes, rabbiting on about how much they'd had to drink and dancing to Strapped In with him as though their backsides were on fire.

When Ben took her out on the floor for a slow number, she thought how she'd never danced with John before. Then she smiled thinking how long it might take for the Strapped In sound to replace Slim Dusty at the Whitemark Hotel.

Later, while Ben talked and laughed and danced on with others, a boy, and moments later, a girl came up and asked her to dance. She apologised to both, saying her asthma was playing up. Then she stepped back into the shadows and gave Ben more space to slip away with a new find, if that's what he wanted to do.

He stayed, though, and after an hour came looking for her – animated and hot and minus his water bottle. 'New starts can begin slowly,' he said in the car after they left the Shark's Tooth. 'So I'll take you home now if that's where you really want to go.' His close, hope-stricken face told her he had another place in mind.

'Yes, thanks.'

He'd ring her again in the morning, he said brightly in front of her place. There was that about him too – off the drugs, he never sulked. There was always tomorrow. Pete was so right. Ben and John barely occupied the same planet.

She leaned over and kissed him softly. 'Thanks, Ben. I enjoyed it.' What went through her mind then was – You can ring me anytime. I'll always want to talk to you, or walk along St Kilda beach or the bike track with you. But nowhere else, not any more, Ben. Beyond those places, our worlds divide. But she couldn't say that to him: not yet. He'd had his best night out in months, even if it hadn't quite finished the way he would have liked – well, at least up to this stage of the evening, anyway.

He beamed back a perfect smile. 'A different affair from the last time we were supposed to go out together, huh, Jack?'

'I was thinking that.' She waited.

'It's good to know the future's ours again, isn't it?'

The door creaked when she opened it and stepped out. 'I might not be here in the morning when you ring.'

'No dramas. I'll try again in the afternoon.'

27

'When do you plan to start looking for work?' her mother asked the next morning, over a slow Saturday breakfast.

'Today, Mum.'

'Will you start with Burger King?'

'I suppose.'

Her mother was a different person in the mornings. It wasn't just that she was sitting down – mirror and make-up free – and clinging to her coffee mug rather than David. Her speech and movements were slower. Her eyes lingered on things as if they offered up choices and she was making decisions about them. With just her daughter there to keep her company, there was no one around to audition for, so silent thoughts occupied most of her time. Jackson recalled a portion of her assigned recitation and analysis lines from *As You Like It*, the Shakespeare comedy her grade twelve English Lit class studied months earlier.

> All the world's a stage,
> And all the men and women merely players:
> They have their exits and entrances;
> And one man in his time plays many parts...

She'd thought of Ben when she first read that: her mother too with her 'exits and entrances' for David. Though Shakespeare obviously hadn't met the one-part specialist vets on Flinders Island.

Flinders filled her thoughts now. Certain things that had happened there would, of course, be forever closed to discussion.

But Pete's Easter job offer wasn't one of them. If she did decide to go back to Flinders, it would be best for her mother to know well beforehand.

'Pete wants to open his Flinders restaurant up again at Easter,' she said, hoping that her mother would work out what that might mean on her own.

'Oh, right.'

'They' re expecting lots of tourists there.'

'The number of tourists Flinders gets in a year, Melbourne gets in a day.' Her mother finished her coffee and went to the sink to put the kettle back on. 'I'm sure Burger King, or wherever you're working, will give you all the working hours you can handle then.'

Getting the message across, subtly, wasn't going to be as easy as she'd hoped.

An hour later, Jackson found herself outside Burger King's front door, but she hesitated going in, and continued on up Swanston Street. Strangely, amongst all the people and street noise, her senses skipped back and picked up the sound of wind rattling the window frames, the slap of waves, shrieking gulls, running sunlight and cloud shadow and the warm sand under her feet. She'd only been away from Melbourne for six weeks and now she felt like a visitor here. She'd adjust; she knew that. All this would feel normal to her again in a few days' time.

Her thoughts played close-ups of John, and yes, of Pete too.

'If the sketch includes us, I'd like to be around when you do it. Just in case your memory wants refreshing.'

'There's an old saying about someone who becomes the fabric of another person's life.'

'I'm only eighteen.'

'I guess the question is how much John's become the fabric of your life? '

'What about tomorrow? '

'What about tomorrow?' she blurted out, unintentionally. She glanced around to see if anyone heard… No; or if anyone had, it wasn't worth registering.

She thought again about her mother and David and that idea about the mind being more important than the eye, and by living in the mind being able to create a world of possibilities, or perhaps in her case, an island of them. From the stories she'd been told there was little doubt her mother's eyes for her 'five-star spunk of a young Mel Gibson husband' had been as all consuming as her own eyes had been for Ben. True, there was the twenty-seven-year age gap between mother and daughter. And yes, at eighteen, she could hardly be classified as a relationship expert. But what she did know was that shy, awkward, one-track John filled her mind now even more than he did when she was on Flinders. She saw him, heard him, felt him and even talked out loud to him here. Besides, going back at Easter would hardly be a life-changing experience. She'd only be there for nine or ten days. She knew what to expect and where she wanted to go, other than to The Sandman's and Patriarch Inlet, of course: the hotel, Strzelecki, Cameron Inlet and…well, the cove…if the beach tent were still up…and it was warm and sunny…and an offer was made… and things felt right. Though visits to a proposed housing site at Trousers Point, or the viewing of house plans anywhere on the island, would be completely off the itinerary.

Her mind struck on another idea. It had been three years since she and her mother had been anywhere together, and 'anywhere' then was Bushed Out. So what if her mother took time off work over Easter and they went to Flinders together? David could come too, even if it was only for part of the time. After all, once she'd had that talk with her mum about living arrangements, the three of them were going to have to learn to live together, weren't they? Though how David would adapt to driving a Bowman Beetle around the island might be cause for concern. Still, her mother wouldn't flinch from driving one: she had before.

Of course, it meant taking the chance that Bowman and Constable Mitchell hadn't said anything they'd vowed not to. If they had, though, and the story got back to Pete or Aunt Louise, she knew they'd squash it. As for John, well, if by Easter their feelings for each other were still strong, and word hadn't got out about why she'd really gone to Flinders in October, she might tell him. Dispense with the need for deception. Test his feelings in the face of an ugly home truth. Ensure their relationship future – if there was to be one – stayed shock-proof. Then again, was it really necessary to do that? What about that mind versus the eye idea she'd been considering earlier? Truth can hurt. Illusions are not always such bad things, especially when they serve to protect people's feelings. So why make things complicated? Why not take a lesson from Ben on this one? Lock up the book on blinks in the past and aim straight for the big bright future.

Jackson got out her long-unused mobile and rang home. When her mother answered, she said in a single breath, 'Mum, this is Jackson. What I didn't tell you this morning was there's a job waiting for me at The Sandman's over Easter and I want to take it.' There, she'd said it.

'Yes, I suspected as much.'

Why she suddenly experienced a tear rush mystified her. She recalled the same thing happening at Pete's that first day back there in January, and thought she must be suffering from prolonged hormone overload. 'And Mum, I was thinking you might take some time off work and come with me. I'd *really* like you to.'

Her mother stayed quiet for a few moments. 'Actually, there was more I should have said too this morning. Like not wanting to spend so much time so far away from you again. So, if that's what you want to do, and you don't mind your old mum cramping your style over there, then okay, I'll have a word to the work gurus about getting some time off.'

'That's great, Mum.' It wasn't just the exits and entrances for David. No way. Her mother played another role much more effectively, that of being who she primarily was – her mother. And Jackson thought then that she would prefer it if David didn't move in. She liked having her mother to herself, especially in the mornings. Still, once she left home, who'd be there for her mother if it weren't him? 'Maybe David could get some time off as well,' she added, knowing she should.

'Maybe. That'll be up to him. But with him or without him, it'll be good to catch up with a few people over there, like Louise. That Pete fellow sounds interesting too. And I wouldn't mind meeting the young vet science student you were telling me about. What's his name again?'

'John.' Jackson smiled picturing David and John discussing wombats and MX5s together.

'Yes, him… Have you gone into Burger King yet?'

'No, but I'm about to.'

'You'd best tell them about our Easter plans. If they don't like the idea, you can always think about staying unemployed and living frugally, at least until we get to Flinders. Your university studies certainly wouldn't suffer for it. Anyway, depending on how you go, we can talk about all this when you get home.'

'We can. Thanks, Mum.'

'Thank you…for the invitation.'

No sooner had she hung up than her mind took flight again. *John, this is Jackson. How are you?… Oh good, good. Are you still going back to Launceston on Monday?… Right. Looking forward to it?… Right.'*

A tram rumbled by, temporarily pulling her mind back before it took off again.

'I guess why I'm ringing is that I want to come back there at Easter… Hold on, just let me finish. And the only way I'll do that is if I know you'll be there and I can work at The Sandman's… Okay good, just checking… I know what he said, but I still want to ring and confirm it with him… Okay… I've missed you too. Heaps… John, please, just one holiday period at a time. There's one other thing I've been thinking about. Have you been up to the cove to get the beach tent yet?… Oh, well, that's up to you.' A smile broke out all over her face. *'What's the water temperature there like at Easter?… That warm, huh?… I know, I know… Yes, I'll ring when I know, I promise. Talk to you soon… John, I'm going now. Bye.'*

She'd tell him about her mother coming over later.

She saw a row of three grounded telephones across the road. She stowed her mobile and checked her watch: eleven o'clock. He'd be down at Lady Barron now.

EPILOGUE

Years later

Tourists continue to visit Flinders, usually in summer. Many stay at the Whitemark Hotel on weekend package tours. Some of the more energetic ones climb Mt Strzelecki. The next day they might head north to Wyabelena for a history lesson, and on to the towering granite headlands at Killiecrankie to look for gemstones. Satisfied they've 'done the island', they fly out with the souvenirs and videos, sketches and photos they'll share with family and friends back home.

Occasionally, though, visitors will cast a curious eye over the crayfish map behind the hotel's front bar. They might ask about the thin line that meanders east and isn't shown on the pamphlets they've read. Depending on whom they talk to, the answer might be –

'Better take out extra insurance on the Beetle.'

'There're potholes out there big enough to bury sheep.'

'I suggest you stick to the more salubrious surroundings of the west coast.'

And that's when you can pick them, the ones who have a tendency to live in their imaginations from the ones who don't. 'I might give it a look,' or 'Looks interesting,' those who do often say.

After arriving at Patriarch Inlet, they'll scan the sea and sand, and gaze at the lagoon alive with birds. Seeing the shack on the headland to their right, they might be heard to say, 'I wouldn't mind spending some time in that shack with a few beers, a roaring fire and a good book or two.'

If by chance they're out there late afternoon on a Thursday, with their imaginations firing, along the shoreline they'll see a barefooted young woman – her fashionable slacks rolled up to her knees – and a dark-haired, freckle-faced little boy searching the sand. A baby wombat will be close on their heels, and a white-bearded old man and a stiff-legged old dog will be doddling along behind. The little boy will bend down, collect a shell and study it closely before reaching up to give it to the woman. If the sea breeze hasn't got up, the visitor might hear the little boy say, 'It's a really good one, isn't it, Mum?'

'Yes, yes it is,' she'll reply, putting the shell in the bag she's carrying.

The little boy will collect more shells as he closes in on the birds. Then he'll hear them, 'Chit-chit-chit,' and see them bill probing the sand. He'll stop. His blue eyes will grow large with wonder. He'll point a finger at them and then look around for the old man, a little impatient for him to catch up. 'Red-necked stints, aren't they, Pete?'

Pete might chuckle with pleasure then. 'They are, yes.'

'Wick-ham, wick-ham.'

The little boy will spot a black and white, orange-beaked bird stalking the shoreline. 'Pied oyster-catcher.'

'I don't have my glasses with me,' Pete will say, 'but I've no doubt that's what it is.'

They'll move on, sea gulls rising and falling again behind them.

Minutes later the boy will squint over the water, pointing. 'Babel Island. Mutton-birds go there and they…they…' He'll look at Pete with a puzzled look. 'What do they do again?'

'Mate for life.'

'Yes, that.' Not concerned with what 'that' might mean, yet, the little boy will continue searching, pointing and calling out to check that he's got his names for things right. Then he'll turn around and look appealingly up into his mother's eyes. 'Can we go far and see if we can find some nautilus shells, Mum?'

She'll study the sea and sky as Pete looks on. 'I don't know if we're dressed for it, Jacob. It's certain to cool down soon.'

'We'll be right.' Jacob will point to his beanie, then to his red 'KOALA BARE – AUSTRALIA' windcheater. 'Grandmum and David gave me these so I won't get cold.'

'We can't be late. I've got assignments to mark and you know your father and I are helping out at The Sandman's tonight, that you and wombat will be staying over at your granddad's.'

'But Granddad loves nautilus shells. So *please*, just a little bit far.'

'All right,' Jackson will say, feigning impatience. 'But only for another ten minutes.' She'll pick up her son, wrap her arms around him and carry him slowly along so that Pete doesn't lag behind.

And Jacob will continue to point and natter away before turning to her again, his face alight, and saying, 'The beach is a beauty, isn't it, Mum?'

Pete will hear Santi then and Jackson will look over at him with a knowing smile. 'Yes,' she'll say to her son. 'Yes, it is.'